Also by Richard M. Jones

The Great Gale of 1871
Lockington: Crash at the Crossing
Capsized in the Solent: The SRN6-012 *Disaster*
End of the Line: The Moorgate Disaster
Collision in the Night: The Sinking of HMS Duchess
Royal Victoria Rooms: The Rise and Fall of a Bridlington Landmark
RMS Titanic: *The Bridlington Connections*
The 50 Greatest Shipwrecks
Britain's Lost Tragedies Uncovered
The Burton Agnes Disaster
When Tankers Collide: The Pacific Glory *Disaster*
The Diary of a Royal Marine: The Life and Times of George Cutcher
The Farsley Murders
Living the Dream, Serving the Queen
Boleyn Gold (Fiction)
Austen Secret (Fiction)
Gunpowder Wreck (Fiction)
Around the World in Shipwreck Adventures
Cretil the Cat (Children's book)

Lost at Sea in Mysterious Circumstances

Lost at Sea in Mysterious Circumstances

Vanishings and Undiscovered Shipwrecks

Richard M. Jones

PEN & SWORD
HISTORY

First published in Great Britain in 2023 by
Pen & Sword History
An imprint of Pen & Sword Books Limited
Yorkshire – Philadelphia

ISBN 978 1 39904 621 3

A CIP catalogue record for this book is
available from the British Library

Typeset by Mac Style
Printed in the UK by CPI Group (UK) Ltd, Croydon, CR0 4YY.

Pen & Sword Books Limited incorporates the imprints of After
the Battle, Atlas, Archaeology, Aviation, Discovery, Family History,
Fiction, History, Maritime, Military, Military Classics, Politics,
Select, Transport, True Crime, Air World, Frontline Publishing, Leo
Cooper, Remember When, Seaforth Publishing, The Praetorian Press,
Wharncliffe Local History, Wharncliffe Transport, Wharncliffe True
Crime and White Owl.

For a complete list of Pen & Sword titles please contact

PEN & SWORD BOOKS LIMITED
47 Church Street, Barnsley, South Yorkshire, S70 2AS, England
E-mail: enquiries@pen-and-sword.co.uk
Website: www.pen-and-sword.co.uk
or
PEN AND SWORD BOOKS
1950 Lawrence Rd, Havertown, PA 19083, USA
E-mail: Uspen-and-sword@casematepublishers.com
Website: www.penandswordbooks.com

Dedicated to the crew of *Foxtrot 4*

'Explicit Nomen'

Contents

Introduction

One of the most fascinating subjects to inspire the imagination is that of the shipwreck; for generations a tale of lost treasure and diving on lost ships was enough to inspire any child with a thirst for adventure. I should know – I was one of them. From an early age the stories of the famous shipwrecks like *Titanic* and *Bismarck* meant that I spent many hours growing up with my head buried deep in a book or glued to the TV screen, captivated by the documentaries or films on these stories of the sea. As time went by the names of thousands of shipwrecks became as familiar to me as football players are to the sporting enthusiast.

Great shipwreck hunters have shown the world that nothing is truly lost. Robert Ballard located *Titanic*, *Bismarck*, USS *Yorktown* and dozens more, David Mearns found the *Derbyshire*, HMS *Hood* and the hospital ship *Centaur* and a team sponsored by the late Microsoft billionaire Paul Allen gave us a host of Second World War wrecks in deep water such as the USS *Lexington*, USS *Hornet*, USS *Wasp* and many others. But there are still many more that are undiscovered. What is even more interesting is that even today there are subjects that seem still to be shrouded in complete mystery. What if I said there was a passenger ship that hit an iceberg on her maiden voyage and sank mid-Atlantic, for example? Many would instantly think of the famous *Titanic*, but many people do not realise that it happened again to the smaller Danish passenger ship *Hans Hedtoft*, only this time all hands were lost.

As the books on the library shelves talk about those that are well known, the ones that vanished without trace only seem to appear in books that entertain the concept of the Bermuda Triangle in the 'mind, body and spirit' section. The people who go missing during a wartime mission are found in the biography sections talking about their lives with a brief statement on their disappearance. Any others may be found in a book detailing dozens of other incidents such as the USS *Oklahoma* at Pearl Harbor, but focusing on the sinking during the 1941 Japanese attack and the deaths that day rather than her eventual salvage and later loss. This is where my writing is different: I will not entirely focus on what has already been written; instead, I will give a brief history of the incident, followed by the circumstances that led to the vessel, aircraft or people being missing to this day.

But the focus on ships only takes up around two thirds of the book, for who could resist a chapter on an abandoned lighthouse, a vanished airliner, a polar explorer or even record-breaking aviators? By the time you have finished reading this, at least one may have already been found – that is the nature of the exploration of the seas during this day and age where technology makes a sea search so much more possible.

In 2021 I published *The 50 Greatest Shipwrecks*, a brief history of what I considered were the most remarkable and historic wrecks of all time. One chapter was about Shackleton's famous Polar expedition which led to the loss of his vessel *Endurance* which, I wrote at the time of writing, had never been found. Just months after the book's publication the first images of the wreck of the *Endurance* were beamed around the world. Remarkable photographs of the name of the ship preserved in picture perfect detail, the ship's wheel forever in one position, the crushed but upright wreck ending a mystery lasting 107 years. For decades there had been expeditions and planned searches but all had failed until now; I have no doubt that many of the mysteries in this book will one day be solved and we will look upon the wreckage of many once-lost shipwrecks.

Whenever there are mysteries such as these, there will be conspiracy theories and alternative explanations as to what occurred and when. With limited information on many of these subjects, it is no wonder it causes an over-active imagination amongst some people, but the last few years have proved that the phenomenon known as the Bermuda Triangle is nothing more than an area of sea where there have been some ships lost without explanation. With the development of GPS trackers and sea safety regulations, a ship such as the *El Faro* would have been just another disappearance on this list a century ago. When she sank with all thirty-three crew in 2015 the wreck was located and the cause of the sinking established. Ships becoming victims of the Triangle in this day and age simply do not exist, if the people of the early twentieth century had the technology we have today they would have reached the same conclusions as we do now. Again, we can prove this by the amount of speculation about the disappearance of the SS *Cotopaxi*, which vanished in 1925 and was recently identified as one of the many wrecks off the coast of Florida that had succumbed to a storm. Doing proper research would have shown that the ship sent a distress call at the time saying that it was taking on water and in trouble. In this case the ship was featured in the science fiction movie *Close Encounters of the Third Kind* which showed it becoming a victim of aliens beaming it up and dropping it into the desert: not that this was a common theory, but you can see how far the minds wander when all the information isn't known (and, yes, some alien abduction theories for the Triangle are serious explanations for a few people).

So, what is it that draws people to want to know more about an incident that is shrouded in mystery? Well, it is the same inquisitive nature that has you seek out a detective drama on the TV or allows you subconsciously to be attracted to the headlines in a newspaper that will sensationally claim to have found something that has long been lost. The disappearance of people tends to make headlines if they vanish in suspicious circumstances – with thousands of people not returning home each year the papers would be full of it on a daily basis. But the names of Madeleine McCann, Suzy Lamplugh and Claudia Lawrence continue to be front-page news whenever a new twist to the tale is written. The sensationalism of the rumours, the mistakes made by the detectives and suspicions of those closest to the victim all fuel the train of thought that ends with one simple conclusion – that nobody knows what really happened.

Only time will tell what really went on as the Malaysian Airlines Boeing 777 went off course in 2014 and was never seen again. Historic investigations are all we have to find out the facts surrounding the crew of the infamous brig *Mary Celeste* over a century before. But still there is no hard evidence that would allow investigators to reach a definitive conclusion, thereby closing the case forever.

But while the drama of the case is played out in the newspapers, on TV, even in the cinema, too many people forget that in each case there were human lives involved. The incidents described in this book involve thousands of people who have died: each person will have had a family, friends, lovers, acquaintances, colleagues and, in some cases, fans. From the celebrity status of band leader Glen Miller to the sinking of the landing craft *Foxtrot 4* thousands of miles from home, we can now revisit these lives and pay tribute to those who are lost forever at sea.

Until of course they are found. Expeditions are being planned every day to seek out those things that elude us. Search teams have already found missing treasure ships, sunken warships and entire vessels from thousands – yes, thousands – of years ago, many of them in excellent condition for the sea can be a preserver of history as well as a destroyer. With the advancement in technology, be it satellites and tracking equipment to sonar and remotely-operated vehicles, there is a possibility and a hope that many of the stories in this book will have a different ending in years to come.

The loss of *Foxtrot 4* is one that is close to me in several ways. I have spoken to those who have suffered as a result of the loss of this vessel in 1982. Their ability to carry on in their efforts to ensure that their loved ones are remembered is the reason that I dedicate this book to the six who died and the eleven who lived. Although the location of the lost craft remains elusive to this day, the memory of the crew lives on.

There is a lot of history still out there to find. It is only a matter of time before we can once again gaze upon a vessel that was once proudly sailing the oceans until it was lost forever beneath the waves.

Part I
The Missing

Chapter 1

Atlantis – A Continent Lost?

The concept of a lost continent has always been speculated for generations – thousands of years in fact. An entire land mass in the middle of the Atlantic Ocean swallowed up by a sudden catastrophic event that is talked about on both sides of the world. The truth is that Atlantis most likely never existed, a figment of the imagination coupled with the romanticised image of a city under the sea where temples still stood in all their glory and statues of gods promoting glory to a land that had long ago ceased to exist other than on the pages of the Jules Verne novel *20,000 Leagues Under the Sea*.

The truth is far less glorious, unfortunately. But this is not to say that evidence of lost cities, islands and towns didn't exist and, in these cases, form the basis of a 'type' of Atlantis. Let's take, for example, Spurn Point in the River Humber, East Yorkshire. Once upon a time this area was a thriving community of villages and towns; a thousand years ago there were churches, houses, markets and farms where people lived and worked just like they do today. But coastal erosion, sinking land masses and general sea conditions had made places like the small town of Ravenser Odd now nothing more than part of the seabed. But this place *did* exist. If this happened right under the noses of the folk from Yorkshire, then what is to say that it didn't happen on a much larger scale somewhere else?

Let's look at an example of the devastation that could literally sink an island. In the year 1883 the volcanic island of Krakatoa near Java, Indonesia, started erupting and caused many of the nearby islands' residents to be rightfully concerned. At 6,000 feet above sea level, the volcano was a formidable sight and evacuations of the surrounding areas then commenced; after all it had been hundreds of years since this volcano had shown any signs of activity. But as the explosions from May of that year became more worrying, the worst was yet to come when on 26 August a catastrophic explosion ripped into the volcano and continued into the following day, the noise being heard over 2,000 miles away. Just forty-eight hours after the first major explosion, the island was silent. Over this short period of time the entire land mass had sunk and was replaced by a smaller island that later rose up to take its place.

The legend of Atlantis was further brought to light in the writings of Greek philosopher Plato in his works named *Timaeus* and *Critias* whereby the Greeks and Atlanteans were at war and the latter mounted an invasion of Athens only to be defeated and lost beneath the waves after making the gods angry. This was all explained in around the year 360 BC, of course many thousands of years after 'the event', but where he got his information from is anybody's guess. What also allows us to believe his story to be fictional is that the people of Atlantis were half-man, half-god, that the island itself was full of immense riches, basically a paradise. Those who study the works of Plato do not consider his story to be true in any way, but then why do so many believe it to this day? Why has the name of this long lost fictional place become synonymous with legend? Could it be based on fact after all?

Well, firstly there is never a true location for Atlantis, other than the mid-Atlantic, but this could be interpreted in so many ways considering that a map of the world was still very much based on only what had been explored at the time. America was nowhere to be seen thousands of years ago and exploration of the ice caps was a long way off. So did confusion reign with other volcanic islands that also bear resemblance? For example, the island of Santorini in the Mediterranean.

Around 1600 BC the volcano that rose into the mid-Aegean suddenly erupted and not only destroyed the island but triggered earthquakes and tsunamis that swept through much of the eastern Mediterranean. This is said to be one of the largest volcanic events in history and is significant in the Atlantis story since the whole story is reminiscent of the lost continent, the size of the island being the only thing that is really different. The fallout of the eruption was felt around the neighbouring countries and is even said to have caused a change in climate as far away as China.

So what evidence is there that there could have been a real Atlantis in the middle of the Atlantic Ocean? Well very little; for a start, the Mid-Atlantic Ridge rips the entire ocean bed up from top to bottom as the tectonic plates shift Europe and America that little bit farther away from each other every year; according to studies published by *National Geographic* this is around one inch per year. As the American lands were not known about in Europe thousands of years ago it is highly unlikely any kind of island would be classed as being 'between the continents'.

But this does not stop Atlantis being considered real, as the evidence suggests there have been events that match the story, albeit a lot smaller in comparison. It has featured in countless books, films, cartoons and even the popular TV science-fiction series *The Man From Atlantis*, proving that the romanticising of the lost continent still thriving beneath the waves is good enough for entertainment value as well as for the fans of superheroes such as comic-book character Aquaman. There are many theories which also include Antarctica being a candidate, where Atlanteans lived until the axis of the Earth changed and the land froze over, not to mention the fact that similar structures on continental Africa have also appeared in South America (pyramids, for example) leading many to believe that they were once joined between the two by a vast land mass.

Whatever happened in history thousands of years ago, the theory of Atlantis does make an interesting story, especially when you consider the real life catastrophic events that have occurred in recorded memory. But for anybody searching for underwater temples and statues of gods in mid-Atlantic, they may be sorely disappointed.

Chapter 2
Cleopatra's Needle

London, the capital city of England and the United Kingdom of Great Britain and Northern Ireland, has for centuries been the place where incredible things have happened and amazing structures built. From the iconic dome of Sir Christopher Wren's St Paul's Cathedral to the more modern-day Shard building, this city has a long history of unique sights that attract millions of tourists from around the world.

One of these structures that is well known by both name and reputation is Cleopatra's Needle, an obelisk 68-feet high and weighing around 224 tons. It was in the early 1800s that the world seemed to be gripped by Egypt fever; everything from ancient statues and parts of a Pharaoh's collection were being shipped around the world by explorers who showed off their finds in museums that, in some cases, are still there.

The London obelisk was originally built in the city of Heliopolis around 1500 BC and later moved north to the port city of Alexandria where over time it collapsed, most likely due to an earthquake that had toppled the famous Pharos lighthouse. There it lay broken in the sand and buried until the British showed an interest in it in 1801, following the successful removal of French troops. A plan to ship it to Britain was never carried out, but in 1820 it was gifted to King George IV anyway by the Egyptian ruler Muhammad Ali Pasha, although this, too, did not end up having the structure moved due to the enormous cost and impracticalities.

During the Great Exhibition of 1851 there was a renewed interest in the obelisk and the two countries agreed a plan to ship it to Britain by 1877. Three civil engineers, brothers John and Waynman Dixon along with Benjamin Baker, designed a vessel that would hopefully bring the obelisk from Egypt and sail it all the way through the Mediterranean and into the Atlantic. The vessel was a barge made of a cylinder containing watertight compartments. The structure was inside this cylinder and the craft was built up around it like a ship – with sails on a mast, a pump, anchors, and a crew of seven. By September of that year the obelisk was inside its new housing and floating free, setting sail from the harbour at Alexandria on

29 September. The barge had been given the name *Cleopatra*, with the steamship *Olga* being the one to tow it home. This was the first time the obelisk had left its home country, over 3,000 years after it was constructed in ancient Egypt.

The voyage through the Mediterranean was slow and steady, taking two weeks to pass through from east to west, through the Straits of Gibraltar and into the Atlantic Ocean. The first leg of the journey completed, *Olga* and *Cleopatra* turned north and set their sights for Britain, but this part of the journey was not going to be as easy. The Bay of Biscay has long had a reputation for being a terrible place to be caught in a storm as evidenced by many ships' logs. Storms whipped up there always seemed worse than if they were in mid-Atlantic with thousands of ships lost over the years. On 14 October 1877, with waves smashing into the two ships and howling winds throwing those on board around, the crew of the *Cleopatra* thought that it was only a matter of time before the barge sank beneath them and the *Olga* decided to attempt a rescue of the seven crew. As the boat was launched and headed over to the *Cleopatra* it was swamped and smashed about in the waves and sank, drowning all six people on board who had been sent to conduct the rescue.

A second boat was sent out and was successful, the barge being abandoned to sink while the *Olga* tried to locate the six missing crew. As they realised that there was no hope for them, *Cleopatra*, too, was lost, believed sunk.

It was several days later that a vessel named *Fitzmaurice* was making her journey towards Valencia in Spain when it came upon a strange-looking vessel wallowing alone in the now calmer seas. It was the *Cleopatra*, somehow still afloat and able to be towed to safety. For the crew of the *Fitzmaurice* this meant a guaranteed prize money for the salvage, so the crew hooked her up and brought her alongside the port of Ferrol. After several months of wrangling over the salvage fee, an agreement was reached and the *Cleopatra* was made seaworthy once again, finally getting under tow on 15 January 1878, this time under the watchful eye of the paddle-ship *Anglia*. On board *Cleopatra* was Captain Carter who had piloted her out from Alexandria, making the final part of the journey, albeit three months late.

Less than a week later, on 21 January, the *Anglia* and *Cleopatra* were sailing up the River Thames into East India Dock, London where it was finally landed after a journey lasting four long months and being almost eight decades in the making. The obelisk was nicknamed Cleopatra's Needle, a name that has stuck ever since, and on 12 September that year it was raised into position at Victoria Embankment overlooking the River Thames.

The craze surrounding anything Egyptian didn't go away for quite a while, especially when expeditions were still finding treasures, history and even inspiration for fashion based on ancient Egypt. This was elevated in 1922 when British archaeologist Howard Carter discovered the tomb of Tutankhamun in the Valley of the Kings, along with the largest collection of Pharaohs' treasures ever seen. With the British Museum host to many other fascinating objects such as the Rosetta Stone, it would feed those hungry for history for many decades to come. But it was not just Britain that was bitten by the Egypt bug, Cleopatra's Needle was actually one of two obelisks in the same site; the second was secured for the city of New York in 1877, being transported across the Atlantic and erected in Central Park four years later. This structure also carries the same nickname as its London counterpart.

For those who visit London today, it is worth a look to see this piece of ancient times standing proud in such a modern city. Despite the neglect in its home country and the battering it had taken getting to Britain, it remains a remarkable feat of building and transportation. Millions of people have gazed up at this marvel of Egypt since it was placed in its current location; it survived a bombing raid nearby during the First World War and to honour those who lost their lives in the sinking of the boat in the Bay of Biscay a plaque was placed at the foot of the structure. This is a great tribute to the men who died in the struggle to get this incredible piece of history to its new home while bravely risking their own lives to save their fellow sailors. Despite most people not knowing the story of the *Cleopatra*, their names will now live on at the base of one of the most famous historic monuments in London. The plaque reads:

William Askin	Michael Burns
James Gardiner	William Donald
Joseph Benbow	William Patan

Perished in a bold attempt to succour the crew of the obelisk
ship 'Cleopatra' during the storm October 14th 1877

Chapter 3

The *Mary Celeste*

Few ships in history provoke a reaction of wonder like that of the *Mary Celeste*. For many the basics are known: that a ship was found abandoned at sea one day and nobody knew what happened to the crew. The mispronunciation of Mary to sound like 'marry' has been a constant factor in the telling of the tale, along with the false facts, conspiracy theories and fictional interpretations that have been used in various books and films.

So we will go back to the original story to get the true facts of what happened. The *Mary Celeste* was a brigantine making a transatlantic journey from New York to Genoa, Italy and had set sail from her anchorage on 7 November 1872. There was nothing particularly special about this vessel, originally launched in Canada in 1861 as the *Amazon*; she changed owners several times and had a bit of a chequered history, her captain becoming ill and dying on her first trip. In 1867 she was run aground, salvaged and sold in 1868 to an American buyer where she was renamed *Mary Celeste* a year later. At 282 tons she could carry a cargo across from America to Europe in just a few weeks, the captain, Benjamin Briggs, highly respected and experienced in sailing this ship.

On board her for this journey was Briggs' wife, Sarah, and their two-year-old daughter Sophia (their son was still at home so that he didn't miss school), as well as a crew of seven sailors. Carrying a general cargo of 1,701 barrels of denatured alcohol, a type of ethanol that is deliberately made to taste and smell terrible to avoid accidental consumption and thereby poisoning anyone unlucky enough to ingest it. *Mary Celeste* weighed anchor and sailed off as soon as the weather allowed. Having been alongside in harbour to load the cargo, the storms had delayed Briggs' journey by forty-eight hours.

On 5 December, around 400 miles east of the Azores in mid-Atlantic, the brigantine *Dei Gratia* was making the same journey across the water to Genoa with a stop off at Gibraltar along the way, under the command of Captain David Morehouse. The ship had set sail on 15 November with a cargo of petroleum and was making steady progress when the helmsman called for the captain to come and check out a ship acting strangely.

The nearby ship, around six miles away, had her sails set rather odd for the weather they were experiencing and, as the *Dei Gratia* edged closer, he saw that it was the *Mary Celeste*, which by now should have been over a week ahead of them and already in the Mediterranean. Nobody was sighted on deck and nobody answered the calls, so it was decided that a boarding party would be sent over to check to see if the crew were alright. The crew members who boarded her searched the ship for any signs of life, but they found nobody at all. The ship was completely abandoned.

Looking around the ghost ship, it was clear that something had happened in the days before; the charts were in a mess around the compartment, the ship's lifeboat was missing, there was enough food to sustain the crew for a very long trip, personal belongings remained where they had been left, a pump had been disassembled and there was just over three feet of water in the bottom of the ship. The cargo of alcohol was intact and there was no sign of what had caused ten people to suddenly vanish into thin air.

Examination of the ship's log showed that the last entry was at 0500 on 25 November, ten days before it was found drifting. The crew of *Dei Gratia* sailed her to Gibraltar where they put a claim in for salvage and answered any questions regarding the finding of the vessel. Suspecting foul play, it took over three months before the insurers paid out to the crew and even that wasn't a full award.

But to this day nobody has ever confirmed what actually happened to the crew of the *Mary Celeste* which has one of the most famous maritime mysteries ever. Countless theories have surfaced, some of them completely ridiculous and some of them involving scientific research. Pirates were ruled out due to the cargo being untouched. Mutiny was suggested, but the crew were trustworthy and would have had no reason to completely abandon the entire ship. A murderous crewmate was ruled out with no evidence of blood, a struggle or any injuries taking place. One more widely held theory is the explosion of alcohol vapours: nine of the barrels were empty and could have leaked over time and ignited, but with no blast damage and scorching this again is highly unlikely. What is more than likely is that it was abandoned on purpose and all ten crew got away in the ship's lifeboat. What we don't know is what could have occurred on 25 November for them to consider this?

At the time of the abandoning the *Mary Celeste* would have been close to land as she passed the Azores, bearing in mind that it was 400 miles away from land by the time it was discovered ten days later. Did the crew try to row their boat towards land and get overwhelmed? Did the flooding down below cause Captain Briggs to risk abandoning ship in the mistaken belief that his vessel was about to sink? Judging by the pump repair attempt (if that is what was going on) then this is probably what happened, but again this is just a likely theory, one of several that could all turn out to be false.

With the story of the *Mary Celeste* world famous, novelists turned their attention to writing works of fiction based on the ship. As the decades went by, the crew of the *Mary Celeste* went down in history as the crew who abandoned the legendary ghost ship. With so little being known, it opened up so much speculation that, in the end, the truth about the actual discovery by *Dei Gratia* was twisted heavily. There was talk of a meal being on the table, still hot (making it look like they had vanished only moments ago) but this is completely false: even if you don't take the temperature of the meal into account there was still no food set out at the table.

Scientific experiments on alcohol explosions for TV documentaries have shown that it is possible for there to be a blast without leaving any damage, but perhaps with 1,701 barrels of alcohol this may not be a fair experiment if you consider what an explosion next to these would bring. Another theory centred on the *Dei Gratia* waiting for the *Mary Celeste* in order to hijack the ship and take the cargo. The fact that the ship sailed over a week after the *Mary Celeste* leaves this theory high and dry. Another historian accuses Briggs of mass murder and suicide, a claim that later led to an apology to the family of Briggs.

So, the truth about the *Mary Celeste* is still unknown. Perhaps it is one of those mysteries that just will never be solved. Maybe one day a historian will find a document that details an unidentified body coming ashore and being buried that would, upon investigation, turn out to be a member of the crew. Until something like this comes up, we can only speculate as to what really happened that day to the *Mary Celeste* and, more to the point, why. With so many theories and written material to sift through it would be a long job to fish out anything new after 150 years.

But the story of the *Mary Celeste* itself does not end there. For she was later sold to new owners and, on one journey in 1879, her captain became ill and died off the island of St Helena. This was the third captain of this ship to die (assuming Briggs and his crew were dead, of course) on a vessel that had already had a cemented reputation of being cursed. She was once again taken over by new owners and ran for several more years as they tried to make a success of her.

Eventually a real conspiracy was taking place whereby the ship was loaded with cheap cargo and over-insured, the captain running her aground deliberately on a reef in Haiti on 3 January 1885. But the captain and his co-conspirators were soon found out and were investigated for fraud. While the courts could not decide a verdict, the captain later died in poverty, another conspirator killed himself and a third went mad. The wreck of the *Mary Celeste* rested on the reef and was never seen again.

In 2001 author Clive Cussler made a big announcement that he had found the wreck of the *Mary Celeste* and it was soon featured on a documentary and in one of his non-fiction books on wreck hunting. However, later analysis of the wood on the wreck dated it to many years after the ship was built and so today the wreck of the *Mary Celeste* is as lost as she has ever been. For a ship as mediocre and plain as this, she has a legacy that has never left the history books.

In the list of most famous mysteries at sea, the story of the *Mary Celeste* and her missing crew still remains firmly in the top place.

Chapter 4

The Lighthouse

There is nothing more lonely than being a lighthouse keeper, or so it has been said. Imagine being out there alone and your only job is to make sure a beam of light keeps shining, possibly a boring job but one that has saved so many lives over the years. Since the ancient Egyptians who built the magnificent Pharos of Alexandria to the civil engineers who constructed the Eddystone Lighthouse on a rock out at sea, the story of the men who built and manned these incredible structures inspired many a film or book. But it is the story of one particular lighthouse with which this chapter is going to deal, one that is shrouded in mystery to this day.

The Flannan Isles are a small group of islands north-west of the Scottish coast, not far from the Outer Hebrides. On one of these islands, Eilean Mòr, stands a lighthouse shining its guiding beacon across the seas as it has done since 1899 when it was first commissioned. Four men would live and work on this barren island to operate the light; three would stay on the island and take it in turns to be the one who would spend time ashore. In December 1900 the three keepers were James Ducat, Thomas Marshall and Donald McArthur, having taken over duty on the 7th to spend the next two weeks on the island.

Everything went fine until, on the night of the 15th, when a passing vessel noticed that the light was not lit, although this ship failed to mention this when eventually going alongside later. With bad weather preventing the sailing of the relief ship *Hesperus*, the crews ready to take over at Flannan Isle did not get to the island until Boxing Day afternoon, but they were very confused. Nobody was there to greet them and the light showed no sign of being on, the island looked in darkness. A rocket was fired and the ship's horn sounded to get their attention but still nothing.

A boat was lowered carrying several of the relief crew and one of the keepers, Joseph Moore, managed to get ashore and head over to the lighthouse. He found the doors locked with the exception of the kitchen entrance where he entered and saw that the whole building was abandoned. The fire had not been lit for days and there was no sign that there had been anything amiss, almost as if the men had walked out to do a job and were due back any moment.

Knowing that something bad had happened, Moore raced back as fast as he could to the boat to get help, the relief crews quickly getting ashore and following him to the top of the rocks in an attempt to get the lighthouse working again while at the same time looking around for any signs of life, but all they found was confusion amongst them. Evidence of the logs showed that the lamp had been extinguished on the early morning of 15 December but had not been re-lit later that afternoon as it should have been. Weather readings had been taken and noted down ready for the log with a time of 0900 that day, so whatever had happened it could be narrowed down to a few hours in the middle of that day.

Confusion reigned. This had never happened before and considering that only one ship seemed to have seen that the light was not working, it had taken eleven days until their disappearance had been noticed. Discussions about where they had gone, where they could be, where was left to search that hadn't already been covered over and over. But it all came back to the inevitable: the three men had been missing for eleven days and nobody had noticed. The only saving grace is that everything seemed to be still working, the lamp was fine and the only thing out of place was that the clock had stopped.

Three keepers stayed on the island to man the lighthouse. In the meantime, an investigation was launched into the disappearance of Ducat, Marshall and McArthur by the Northern Lighthouse Board, but there was not a shred of evidence to say what they had been doing or where they had gone. The only assumption was that they had gone outside to secure equipment in the storm and all three had been washed away into the sea.

As with many mysteries as the *Mary Celeste* has shown us, there are conspiracies galore and so many different theories as to what could have happened to the three keepers. Over the next hundred years they were accused of being spies and picked up by a ship, one murdered the other two and then committed suicide, faking their own deaths to start a new life. All of these are strangely familiar whenever a group of people vanish for no good reason. But the truth is probably much more simple and tragic – that they went out to secure their equipment in the storm and met with an accident.

Part of the island had suffered damage as a previous entry in the log had shown. It was feasible that they would want to make sure that everything was lashed down and wouldn't be damaged. Thomas Marshall had actually been fined five shillings for losing equipment in a previous incident, so this gives credence to him not wanting a repeat of this and perhaps his two colleagues ventured out to help him. Let's face it – you would not want to head outside in that weather on your own. On saying that, though, the clothing that had been left behind showed that one of them had departed wearing sea boots and oilskins, one had taken just a waterproof coat, but McArthur had left his coat behind and could have ventured out wearing only a shirt. Could this be a case of seeing something that required him to rush out to assist and not even having time to put a coat on? We may never know.

But still the story has no true conclusion, but there have been several factual books investigating the disappearance and it also inspired the 2019 movie *The Vanishing* starring Gerard Butler as well as a song by rock group Genesis titled 'The Mystery of Flannan Isle Lighthouse', released on their 1998 album 'Genesis Archive'.

Ironically, the reason there were three people on the lighthouse is because of the incident at the Smalls Lighthouse off the Welsh coast in 1801 when one of them died in a freak accident and the other, fearing blame, went mad with worry over the thought of being accused of his death (they did not get on well and often quarrelled). After that lighthouse keepers would work in threes. In the case of the Flannan Isle Lighthouse, this would never have saved them anyway.

Today the lighthouse is fully automated and has been since 1971, but the island and lighthouse will always be tarnished with the ghosts of the three lighthouse keepers who never returned.

Chapter 5
Admiral Wilcox USN

A shocking fact that has only recently come to light is that hundreds – yes, hundreds – of people have gone missing from cruise ships over the last two decades or so. With the easy flow of alcohol freely available and the ability to simply climb up onto the guard rails, it is no wonder that the possibility of a man overboard is very real. In many cases some of these missing persons are found to have been murdered; an entire series dedicated to this, called *Cruise Ship Killers*, has proved popular, although the name of the ship and the cruise line involved is always omitted.

With the military things are very different. There are not only rules in place and sentries closing up for when such things may occur (for example when two ships replenish at sea using fuel lines) but numerous alarms that (in this day and age) sound an audible siren and drop flares and a Perry Buoy (life ring). This does not alleviate the fact that whenever somebody goes overboard it is never done in a controlled way as you would jump off a diving board and aim to land feet/arms first. It is mostly done accidentally and when that happens you have the element of shock, hitting the sea in a bad way such as landing on your neck or back. In fact, you may end up unconscious and if that doesn't kill you the extreme cold of the ocean soon will.

Even being very close to land and with safety an arm's reach away the body goes into shock and muscles start to seize up before hypothermia sets in. A human body can lose most of its body heat in just a minute; depending on how cold the water is you could be dead within a few minutes. Again, this all depends on the climate, falling overboard in the Caribbean will give you a better chance of survival than going over in the Baltic, but the water still sucks all the body heat out of a person either way. Time is of the essence and the quicker somebody is found to have fallen over the better the chances of survival.

So, when the battleship USS *Washington* was in a task group of other ships on the morning of 27 March 1942 in the middle of the North Atlantic, it was an alert lookout who first spotted something not right in the water. The build-up of ice around the upper decks of the ships meant that it was getting harder to see ahead and the bows of the vessels were constantly smashing into the waves as the fleet battled the cold Atlantic swells. Suddenly, a stern lookout saw a person in the water floating by and the shout of 'Man Overboard' reverberated throughout the ship. Due to the fact that the task force was in strict radio silence, the signal was sent to the other ships by flags and whistle. The search was on for the missing crew member.

Two ships reported seeing a man in the water, one saying that he was swimming towards a life ring, another that he was seen face down. Neither could effect a rescue in time. With the unknown sailor vanishing from sight, the *Washington* had to find out who the missing person was and the captain, H.H.J. Benson, ordered an immediate roll call of the souls on board.

With around 2,000 people, it was no mean feat but when the figures came back it shocked him even more. Everybody was accounted for. He ordered a recount on the chance that there had been a mistake and that somebody had been counted but not checked. But, again, the head count came back with everybody there. Not happy with this and, fearing that a mistake had been made, he went to report it to the Admiral.

Rear Admiral John W. Wilcox Jr was in overall command of the task group, consisting of his flagship, *Washington*, the aircraft carrier *Wasp*, the two cruisers *Tuscaloosa* and *Wichita*, along with eight destroyers. He had joined the navy in 1905 and had seen a large amount of service during the First World War and was now in charge of this fleet for duties in the Second. Outside his door a Marine sentry stood and knocked, but there was no answer. When he opened the door he was shocked to find the cabin completely empty. A full search of the ship was carried out before the inevitable fact was realised – the only man not on the roll-call muster list was the admiral.

A later inquiry heard evidence that Admiral Wilcox had been looking a bit off colour that day and looking confused, with members of the crew saying that they had seen him on the upper deck not long before the man overboard alarm had been raised. They concluded that he had most likely been swept overboard after becoming ill through a heart attack or sea sickness and that no negligence was involved in his death. He was the first admiral in the US Navy ever to be lost overboard at sea. There has only ever been one other and that was from a passenger liner in 1958. Admiral Wilcox died just five days after his sixtieth birthday.

Another tragic part to this story is that, during the search for the missing man, the USS *Wasp* launched aircraft to aid in the search, but one of them crashed into the sea near the stern of the *Wasp* while attempting to land, killing the two crewmen.

While there seemed to be very little that the twelve ships could do for their admiral, his death highlighted the fact that nobody is immune to the powerful wrath of Mother Nature. With the body not being recovered, the fleet continued on their journey to Scapa Flow, a journey that had only begun in Maine the day before and had already lost three people through accidents.

Today there are much better ways to recover a man overboard, the alarms and releases for one; ships of a certain size have some kind of helicopter; a swimmer of the watch can jump in while attached to a rope to physically manhandle a casualty and, of course, the ship's boat can be launched in minutes for a faster rescue. There are stories of people going overboard and floating around for several days alive, but these are few and far between. In the case of Admiral Wilcox, his name will forever live on as the man who vanished in the icy seas while in charge of an entire task force.

Chapter 6

The *Joyita*

For many people the story of the *Mary Celeste* is the one ship that invokes the most mystery since they believe this is the only ship at sea that had the entire crew vanish. But this is not the case, for this has actually happened several times and, incredibly, several of them have been in the modern post-Second World War era, in the age when sea searches could be more thorough and transmission devices could narrow down a search. But for the occupants of the former luxury yacht *Joyita* they might as well have been back in the 1800s.

This vessel was launched in 1931 and owned by movie director Roland West, the 70-foot-long yacht cruising up and down the American coast entertaining guests and allowing its occupants to live the dream in luxury. As the Second World War arrived at the shores of the USA, *Joyita* (pronounced yo-yeeta and meaning 'little jewel' in Spanish) would be put into service as a patrol vessel. After various years that had taken a toll on her structurally, including running aground and having cheap repair work undertaken, *Joyita* survived the war and although some parts were replaced with less-expensive alternatives there was nothing wrong with her and she was later sold to new owners. For several years she was used as a trading and fishing charter vessel in the early 1950s and overall was still in fair condition. One of the things that was noted is that the hull planking was lined with cork, making her very buoyant in the event of any kind of emergency. This would be evident as she made her final voyage.

On 3 October 1955 she set sail from Samoa in the Pacific, with a total of twenty-five people on board, heading for the Tokelau Islands, a journey that would take two days. On board were nine passengers as well as a cargo of medical supplies, but there was nothing dangerous on board and the weather conditions were said to be good. The vessel had a problem with one of the two engines which had to be shut down, but the *Joyita* could manage on one engine and so chugged along seemingly without any further problem.

The voyage itself was just under 300 miles in total and on board were a mixture of local islanders and New Zealanders and she would be due alongside on 5 October. The small boat was only 70-feet-long and 75 gross tons but was a regular at these journeys by now; after all she had been going over two decades and had had her fair share of knocks.

But when word spread that she was overdue on 6 October a search team went out to look for the ship. Aircraft and ships combed the area for six days but not a thing was found that could have given a clue as to the fate of the *Joyita*. With 100,000 square miles of ocean searched, there had been no distress call and no wreckage was found. It was as if the ship had just vanished into thin air.

What happened next shocked everyone. A month later, on 10 November, the cargo vessel *Tuvalu* was making a journey west to the Funafuti Atoll when the crew came upon a ship ahead that didn't seem to be moving. Attempts to call the ship were met with silence as *Tuvalu* moved in to what looked like a small vessel that was semi-flooded and in obvious signs of distress. As they edged closer, the name on the vessel became clear. It was the *Joyita*.

The investigation of this ship showed that the vessel had suffered some kind of incident; there was chaos on board with some cargo missing, broken glass on the bridge, damage to the rooms inside and bloody bandages near a doctor's medical bag. But, above all, there was absolutely no sign of any of the nine passengers and sixteen crew. The vessel carried three Carley life rafts and a dinghy, all of which were missing. The radio was tuned to the distress frequency but the radio itself did not work.

With the vessel itself leaning over and full of water, a pipe that had been repaired during the Second World War was identified as being the source of the flood. The vessel was towed to shelter in Suva, the Fijian capital, where further examination could take place, but other than the disruption on board there were no clues as to what exactly had caused the entire complement of the *Joyita* to vanish. It was clear that they had voluntarily abandoned ship due to the missing rafts and the radio being set to the distress frequency, but what exactly they had experienced was anybody's guess. It is possible that the flooding had created a panic and led to confusion, especially if it was in the middle of the night which is highly likely. The lack of ability to know what is going on, coupled with the human factor of how fear spreads between people, would have led to bad decisions and, most likely, injuries along the way. But where they all went and how the vessel could remain missing for so long when so large an area was searched by the rescue teams was anybody's guess.

Again, there were theories about what happened, including the usual – mass murder, pirate attack, kidnap by Soviets, insurance fraud, mutiny and even an attack by the Japanese (despite the end of the war being a decade previous). All of these bore no fruit with the only evidence being what was found. It is questionable if even today this mystery could be solved but, like the *Mary Celeste*, the *Joyita* now sits on the list of ships found drifting with nobody on board.

The *Joyita* herself was later sold once again and ran aground in 1959. The state of the ship became worse as time went on and she was used as a tourist bureau by a man who wanted to turn her into a museum. This never happened though. Before long she was once again abandoned and stripped of any useful parts that could be salvaged until there was nothing left of her by the 1970s.

Although several books have been written about this ship, she nevertheless remains one of the great sea mysteries of our time but that is largely forgotten when compared to others.

Chapter 7

High Aim 6

Joyita and *Mary Celeste* now seem a lifetime away. Few people remember *Joyita* and nobody is alive who ever saw the more famous of them. But few realise that it still happens today and the next two chapters are going to highlight two similar stories from modern time that have baffled investigators and lead us to ask if we are really any further on to solving these kinds of mysteries than we were 150 years ago?

So now we turn to another similar case but this time it is a completely different type of vessel and one with a sinister twist. This is the story of the Taiwanese fishing vessel *High Aim 6*, a white-hulled 80-foot-long standard vessel which flew the flag of Indonesia, which was familiar to the hunting grounds of East Asia. She left the port of Liuchiu in Taiwan on 31 October 2002 and launched her equipment as usual on reaching the fishing grounds. Everything was going well, the crew were working hard and they had netted a catch that had already started to fill up the holds. The captain spoke to the owners in early December and everything seemed fine. That was the last they heard of *High Aim 6*.

The owners reported her missing in late December and a search got underway covering thousands of miles of ocean, but nothing was found and the crew were presumed to have been lost at sea.

On 8 January 2003 the warship HMAS *Stuart* approached a drifting vessel that had been reported a few days before and attempted to establish communications with it. With no reply, they made a note of the name and prepared to board. The *High Aim 6* had been found, miles away from her last reported position and in calm seas, eighty-two miles off the Rowley Shoals, 160 miles west of Broome, Australia. The fishing vessel was boarded and by the crew of *Stuart* and they were shocked to find not a soul on board.

As the *High Aim 6* was inspected it became clear that something had happened; the crew had caught fish as it was still in the hold rotting away. There was no sign of a struggle on board but any life rafts or lifeboats were missing. The only sign of life was the fact that seven toothbrushes were counted, giving an idea of how many crew should have been on board, with tinned food still in storage. Whatever had gone on, the crew had not starved and drifted without power – there was still half a tank of fuel. A further search found that personal possessions were still onboard but nothing that could give any clue to either identity or fate of the persons involved.

What was even stranger was that, when the vessel was originally sighted on 3 January, the ship was underway but now, five days later, the steering was locked into position and the engine shut down. A calendar had the date of 3 January displayed with previous dates pulled off below it, so was she manned right up until forty-eight hours before the *Sydney* boarded her? With no clue as to what had gone on, the *High Aim 6* was towed to Broome where detectives combed the ship looking for clues.

It was later found that one of the crew members had made several phone calls after the ship had last reported in, and indeed since the discovery. A further search had found that the recruitment agency had hired ten men for the ship but again this didn't give an exact figure when you consider who was already on there and the fact that there were only seven toothbrushes found. Another report said that the captain and engineer had picked up a crew of eight in mid-November. At first it was thought the ship was being used for people smuggling, but the fish in the holds put that theory to rest straightaway.

The next theory was that the ship had been taken over by pirates, but then the ship was abandoned rather than being seized. Again though, if pirates had taken them hostage then where were they held with, so far, no demands? Nothing made sense, no matter which theory was thrown around.

Police in Indonesia eventually located the crew member who owned the phone and found him alive. He confessed that the crew had mutinied and killed the captain and chief engineer on 8 December before they all went back to their homeland. No other explanation was given. At the time of writing, there is still no real explanation as to what happened, why the crew mutinied, how everybody got off the ship and where they are today. Very little information was given out and the discovery of the crewman only threw up more questions than answers. When the police confirmed that the captain had spoken to the owners on 16 December, that throws the date of the murders out by over a week. So, again, who was telling the truth?

What really happened on that vessel during her long period at sea? Did the crew really mutiny or was it a made-up story by an attention-seeking crewman who had left the ship? Why is there so very little information available on this investigation? For the investigators this was just as baffling as for those who originally found her abandoned. Searching a derelict ship must have been horrendous; if the holds were full of fish that had been caught a month ago the smell would have been overpowering. Any search of the holds and subsequent forensic analysis would not have been pleasant by any standards. But whether the truth was being told or not, the fact remained that around ten (possibly more) people were missing but, in this case, not necessarily assumed dead. We can only wonder if more information will be forthcoming as the years go by and new evidence is found.

The *High Aim 6* was abandoned on a Broome beach for over a year. There were plans to use her as an artificial reef for divers but that was discounted when it was found that the hull was too buoyant. Eventually it was broken up where it lay and taken to landfill in October 2004. So ended the strange saga of the *High Aim 6*.

Chapter 8

Kaz II

The final 'missing crew' story of this book is that of the yacht *Kaz II* which joins the ranks of weird happenings at sea, but this is much more recent. It was 15 April 2007 when the white-hulled catamaran slipped its moorings from Airlie Beach in Queensland, Australia and headed out to sea for the trip of a lifetime for brothers John and Peter Tunstead and their mutual friend Derek Batten, all retired and living in Perth. They were heading for Townsville in the first leg of their journey around the coast that would take the 32-feet-long (9.8-metres) yacht from east to west.

The skipper was Derek and he was the only one of the three who had any experience and that was only minimal – a sailing course and a couple of trips on the yacht around the nearby islands. The other two had been on boats since an early age and had been on a volunteer sea rescue crew, but nothing like this before. But this did not deter them as they prepared to live the dream, carrying a case of beer, a supply of food and a .44 calibre rifle with 100 rounds of ammunition just in case. The journey was expected to take around two months.

Less than two hours after leaving port one of the crew had a call from his wife. All was good. That same day Derek held out a video camera while the other two started fishing over the side. Peter Tunstead was sitting on the edge with the guardrail removed not wearing a lifejacket, a foolish thing to do, being a non-swimmer. They talked about 'threatening skies' as they enjoyed what they were doing.

Three days later a passing helicopter near the Great Barrier Reef 100 miles out to sea noticed the yacht seemingly adrift and radioed in to the authorities. A boat was sent out and the *Kaz II* was boarded, but when they got on board and had a look around there was no sign of the three friends. Like the other ships in this book so far, they had vanished from their vessel.

The catamaran was in good working order and nothing seemed to be amiss. A laptop was out and switched on, the engine was running, food and cutlery were set out on the table, all safety equipment was functional and all lifejackets were still on board. It was like the guys had stopped what they were doing and went up on deck for a breather; only in this case they never came back down.

On the upper deck the sail had been shredded and the yacht was missing a life raft, although there is no confirmation that one was even on board in the first place. What was strange was the amount of knives scattered along the floor. This left the search teams nervous in case somebody was hiding after being attacked, although the lack of blood or signs of a struggle put paid to that theory.

With no clue as to the whereabouts of the crew, a search was launched on 18 April with aircraft and seagoing vessels scanning the waves in the hope that miracles did happen. More units joined the search the following day including the volunteer rescue teams around the coasts. But they found nothing and on the 21st in the early evening the search was called off.

So, once again a vessel floating without crew at sea. What could have happened this time? What evidence was there to suggest their fate? The video camera was located and the footage was played back, showing that the *Kaz II* was under sail and that, despite the seas being a bit rough, none of the three were wearing lifejackets. With the data from the GPS showing it drifting later that day, it is evident that the lack of care for safety was the cause of the three men having some kind of accident and being carried overboard as the yacht continued on her journey.

A year later a four-day inquest was held in the Townsville Coroner's Court and they had an incredible 107 pieces of evidence and testimony from twenty-seven witnesses. The skipper's wife confirmed that this was their first sailing boat, but they had been on or around boats for twenty-five years and were usually very safety conscious. The boat itself was in good condition and he had decided to take his two friends with him for safety in case only two people were not enough – as when they had planned to do it as husband and wife.

It was also there that a fishing vessel skipper confessed that he had seen the *Kaz II* drifting on 16 April but, after not seeing anyone on board, left the boat to drift, finding it odd but not odd enough to alert anybody.

The coroner, Michael Barnes, concluded that there was no foul play involved but the three of them did meet with an accident and proposed a scenario whereby the propeller was fouled by a rope trailing behind (which was caught on the video camera) and in turn one of them fell overboard, another going over to help and the third being knocked over by the swinging boom as he was trying to turn the vessel around. Whether this was accurate or not is another question, but this is probably as close as we will get to knowing what really went on that day. Thanks to the video footage and the GPS, it can at least give us a rough idea of the time of incident and clear up a few questions.

The sea is a cruel mistress and if not shown respect will come back and bite you. The lack of safety awareness on a small vessel in choppy seas is something that may only ever give you one opportunity to correct. For all three men to go overboard through pure negligence is both shocking and sad. It would have been the trip of a lifetime for them but instead turned into three missing persons. Their bodies were never recovered.

As with the *Mary Celeste*, *Joyita* and *High Aim 6*, the *Kaz II* has joined these vessels as the mystery ghost ships of the sea, the conspiracy theories once again taking over and rife with rumour: it was pirates, it was an insurance scam, it was murder, it was kidnap; the list is endless. The thorough investigation proves that there was no third-party involvement and the inquest gathering the evidence together put to rest any of the wilder theories. It is safe to say now that what the coroner concluded is most likely what happened. A tragic accident and one that could so easily have been avoided.

What is fascinating when the stories of these four ghost ships are studied is the increase in evidence as the years go by. By the time *Kaz II* is found drifting the investigators are able to consult GPS, video footage and gather together so much evidence that, even if you couldn't say for sure what did happen, you could easily discount what didn't. Had there been the technology of today in the time of the *Mary Celeste*, the mystery would have been solved straightaway – perhaps.

But modern technology or not, the fact remains that this is still a sea mystery and the impossible can still seem to happen; 134 years apart, it would seem that little has changed and that crews can still go missing in the strangest of circumstances. But, like its predecessors, the mystery and tragedy of the *Kaz II* is now forever cemented in the tales of the sea that will be told for many more years to come.

Chapter 9
Jian Seng

Just when you think that it would be impossible for ships to be found randomly abandoned, along comes another one that instantly makes the headlines and leaves the same people flummoxed as to what happened to the crew. Although the story of the *Jian Seng* is quite different and for good reason, for nobody knows where this ship came from.

With any vessel that has been lost at sea or has an incident occur on board, we know the name of the ship, its vital statistics, builders, launch date, owner's details, captain and crew; the list is endless. But on 8 March 2006 a ship was sighted just over 100 miles west of Queensland, off the coast of Australia, by a passing commercial vessel which reported that the small tanker appeared to be drifting. The ship was clearly old, covered in rust and in a fairly bad state, the white superstructure probably the better part of the ship while everywhere else looked as if it had not seen a good day's maintenance in months.

The unknown vessel was not doing anything illegal and so it was left alone but still monitored by a coastguard aircraft for a total of seventeen days before authorities decided to board it. When the Australian customs vessel *Storm Bay* arrived at the scene, they waited until the morning of 24 March to board her and when they got on board found absolutely nothing.

No crew was only the start of this mystery. She had been stripped bare and was just an empty shell of a vessel. Confused members of the boarding team hunted around for anything that could tell them anything, but there was nothing except the possibility that the name of the 262-foot-long ship was *Jian Seng*. Never before has such a sea mystery been to the point of where nobody knows where the ship comes from or where it had been. There was nothing to suggest a port of registry, a nationality or, indeed, if anyone had used this ship for years. The derelict ship seemed to offer very little when it came to clues.

There was no evidence of people smuggling, drug running and cargo carrying whether legal or illegal. The closest theory anybody had for this was that she was being towed for scrap and broke the tow and was abandoned, but again where did this take place? There was no evidence of any violence on board, nor criminal activity, but the identifying marks of the ship had been removed deliberately.

The ship was photographed by the Australian Customs Service who carried out a full search of the mystery vessel to determine anything they could from what they had found on board. A broken tow rope dangling from the bow supported the scrapping theory, but another was that it was being used as a supply ship for fishing vessels after a quantity of rice was found, a rather random thing to find on an otherwise empty ship.

The engine room was examined and found in such a bad state that it would have never worked; the ship would have been without power for a considerable period of time by the time she was found.

An argument broke out in the Australian government when a senator stated that a ship had been ignored for seventeen days when it could have posed a threat to national security, to which it was pointed out that this was not a shipping lane and that taking and diverting resources to a ship that posed no threat would leave the defence capability very thin in areas where it was needed most.

All this time, the *Jian Seng* was towed to the port of Weipa by salvagers where it was checked for hazards and where oily water was removed safely.

By then investigators were puzzled as to what to do with the tanker, with no owners coming forward and no clue as to where it had come from, the decision was taken to scuttle it in deep water. On 21 April 2006 the *Jian Seng* was towed out to sea and sunk, the story of how she came to be adrift off the Australian coast never being determined officially.

Chapter 10

The Bizarre – Lego, Cigarettes ... and Ducks

When I first told my friends about me writing this book, I discussed with them the possibilities of which interesting stories to add. What sort of thing could be classed as being vanished at sea or lost that would stand out above all the rest? What would leave the reader fascinated yet learn something new along the way? Stories of the missing crews have been reported in the press before as have many other of these stories, but one friend sent me a link to a news story that had me thinking just how many bizarre things have not only been lost at sea but years later start to come ashore many miles away from where they were last seen.

There are strict rules regarding things that come ashore. Each piece of cargo or shipwreck can be taken away by the public but must be declared to the Receiver of Wrecks. This office will then endeavour to track down the owner who will either want it back, in which case they must pay the finder a salvage fee, or they will allow the finder to keep it. This was highlighted in a huge way in January 2007 when the container vessel *MSC Napoli* got into difficulty off the south coast of England. Her crew were taken off but eventually she was forced aground to save her from sinking; however, her thousands of containers began falling off the ship in the weather and severe listing.

These containers washed ashore at the nearby Branscombe Beach and suddenly the wreck of the *MSC Napoli* was front-page news as the containers were raided by locals and, in many cases, people who lived many miles away who had heard about the treasure and race to the beach. Within days the beach was a mess of litter and wreckage, the containers being forced open in many cases where photographers from the press were capturing the most unheard of scenes in maritime history as people walked off with brand new motorcycles and, in one case, the contents of someone's house which had been put in a container to move overseas. The whole debate over who owned these items raged on and, eventually, the police were called in to cordon off the beach. Although the rules were to declare the items found (so technically nobody was doing anything wrong taking it from the beach) it was clear that many people had no intention of doing that.

So, when containers wash overboard from one of the huge container vessels (and they are getting bigger by the year) it is inevitable that some will wash ashore and break open. In these cases, there have been some unusual incidents. On 13 February 1997 the container vessel *Tokio Express* was struck by a rogue wave around twenty miles off Land's End and rolled heavily as the ship fought to stay upright. Thankfully the vessel was okay but sixty-two containers were washed overboard. The ship went alongside in Southampton soon after in order to be checked over. But one of these containers contained small plastic toy Lego pieces, which were going to be sea-themed building sets. Ironically, the beaches of the south coast of England were now littered with random Lego sea creatures, scuba divers and flowers. Almost five million pieces were in that container and the next twenty-five years saw this cargo come ashore all along the southern coast, but parts have even washed ashore on the eastern shores of the United States. Today there are people who are monitoring this environmental disaster and regularly hunt the beaches looking for the rare pieces of what has become quite a collection.

I remember an incident at school in the mid-1990s when the cargo ship *Kidira* lost at least two containers off the Yorkshire coast, one of which was full of cigarettes and tobacco products. The beaches at Bridlington and Fraisthorpe were littered with wet packets of cigarettes and, needless to say, it did not take long before word spread that free cigs were out there for the taking. With the product being consumable, it was clear that these were being collected and dried out at people's homes and either smoked by the finders or sold on cheap. Either way the police were arresting anybody who broke the rules, although that didn't stop the finders hunting for more when they could get away with it, nor did it stop them being photographed posing with their finds on the front page of the local *Bridlington Free Press*.

These are not just isolated incidents. It is known that well over 1,000 containers a year are lost from the decks of cargo ships, the worst incident being the *MOL Comfort* in 2013. She sank in the Indian Ocean and many of the ship's 4,293 containers floated away. Every time a container is lost it is not just the contents that are considered, it is the fact that many of them do not sink straight away and, instead, float around, sitting very low in the water. The very small amount that is still visible at the surface is sometimes not enough for ships to see them in time to avoid striking them, which can cause serious damage to a ship's hull. There have been incidents reported of smaller pleasure craft, such as yachts, striking an unidentified object that they had not seen, in some cases causing irreparable damage. With thousands of these containers bobbing around at sea, sometimes for years, is it any wonder that we are not getting more reports of bigger vessels falling victim to these terrors.

The last container-related story I am going to cover is the one that my friend e-mailed me about, although I had heard of it previously. It was on 10 January 1992 that the container vessel *Ever Laurel* was making a journey through the Pacific from Hong Kong to Tacoma, Washington when the storm that it was battling caused twelve of her containers to wash overboard. One of them broke open. It was filled with plastic bath toys called Friendly Floatees – almost 29,000 of them. It is now thirty years since these ducks, beavers, frogs and turtles started their journey and the fact that they were designed as floating child's toys meant that oceanographers could track the currents and progress made, most of all where they ended up. Two reports of ducks coming ashore in Scotland 2003 and Devon 2007 showed that, while the Devon find was not one of them the one in Scotland could be one of the *Ever Laurel*'s. The incredible journey taken by these ducks has inspired books and songs, as well as the ducks now becoming collectors' items. But this highlights just how much pollution is being dropped into the sea from ships and how it can stay within our ecoystem for decades without ever showing signs of degradation. Thankfully, the ducks can float around until recovered. It's the smaller things like the Lego that could be consumed by sea life or sucked into the intakes of marine craft. The fact that scientists can track and use the ducks as a tool for monitoring the oceans is a good thing, but it just shows how far pollution can travel when it is given the time and tide to do so. Whether it is plastic ducks, tobacco or brand new motorbikes, the number of containers lost at sea is rocketing and many thousands of them are still floating about today just waiting to come ashore.

Part II
Warships

Chapter 11

Revenge

'At Flores, in the Azores Sir Richard Grenville lay.' So began the famous opening verse of 'The *Revenge*: A Ballad of the Fleet' written by Victorian poet Alfred Lord Tennyson in 1878. His work was the story of a sea battle that defied all odds and showed Grenville to be a hero of the story – one man and his crew against an entire Spanish fleet.

The galleon *Revenge* was built in Deptford in 1577 and was around 140 feet in length, not a very large ship by any standards but within a decade she had taken part in the famous raid around the Spanish coast led by Sir Francis Drake in what was known as 'singeing the King of Spain's beard'. The year 1588 was the duel with the Spanish Armada where Drake used *Revenge* as his flagship, attacking the fleet off the French coast before storms put paid to the rest of the ships which were sunk all along the Irish coast not long after. Several other expeditions were not successful but, to make sure that the Spanish could not rebuild their navy, it was decided to have a permanent naval presence in the middle of the Atlantic with the hope of intercepting the Spanish treasure ships bringing riches from their colonies back to Spain and providing much needed funding to rebuild their fleet.

In charge of the *Revenge* by 1591 was Sir Richard Grenville, 49 years old and Vice Admiral of the Fleet. He had been raised in political circles and had seen his fair share of action over the years, and not just at sea. His father, Roger, had been captain of Henry VIII's flagship *Mary Rose* and had been killed in the sinking off Portsmouth in 1545.

In his task force Grenville had a number of vessels that had crews who had come down with sickness. This was common in the navy at this time and had been a problem for many years when ships were deployed to foreign lands. Holding out off the Azores, he sent many of the men ashore to get treatment and, by coincidence, it was during this period that the Spanish were found to be heading their way from the east. Many of the ships proceeded to sea as quickly as possible. The incoming fleet was clearly too powerful for the English to be able to take them on alone, but Grenville had decided that he would not leave his position and allow the Spanish to give chase. With the tiny *Revenge* all alone, suddenly this ship was faced with fifty-three Spanish warships heading towards them. With only around 100 crew left on board they got the ship ready to fight. This was nothing more than a suicide mission to save the other ships and allow them enough time to get away, but it was one that would go down in history.

On 31 August 1591 the fleet had arrived to find the single ship ready to do battle. The initial firing on the *Revenge* was unsuccessful due to the skills they had in avoiding the shot. But with such an overbearing amount of firepower aimed on one ship it was only a matter of time before it was hit. As the first rounds smashed into the warship, the ship began to break apart bit by bit. As one ship had finished pounding the *Revenge* another would take its place. Attempts to board were driven off and many members of the Spanish boarding parties were killed.

At this point it was obvious that Grenville and his men were putting up a hell of a fight. No one had expected the battle to last so long, let alone hold the Spanish off for as long as they did. As day became night, two Spanish ships collided and suffered serious damage, one of them sinking. So far, the Spanish losses had been very high and yet *Revenge* fought on.

It was in the early morning of 1 September that the *Revenge* finally surrendered, on condition that the crew's lives would be spared when captured. With her timbers smashed, her crew in terrible condition and Sir Richard Grenville severely injured, the battle was finally over. Grenville succumbed to his injuries two days later.

But the success of the Spanish was short lived as once again Mother Nature was against them. The *Revenge* and her prize crew, along with several Spanish vessels, were caught in a terrifying storm over the next few days and were lost at sea. There were reports of the Spanish being able to salvage guns from the wreck site but, since the 1600s, there have been no reports of the wreck being found.

Sir Richard Grenville and the *Revenge* was perhaps one of the bravest sea fights in history. The impossible odds and the gut determination of those few crewmen against so many Spanish ships defies logic in how they managed to fend them off for so long. It is no wonder that Lord Tennyson wrote about it and that scholars have studied the battle. The selfless act to sacrifice his ship is one that takes a huge amount of courage to carry out with odds at fifty-three to one and a reduced crew.

The battle has also inspired several paintings, the scenes set of a broken and dismasted ship, on fire and with sails draped across the devastated deck but the flags of the Admiral and country still flying. The image of the crew sticking it out until the very last possible moment is at the forefront of the story. Nearby, there is a concentration of Spanish vessels very close to each other giving the viewer no doubt as to the calibre of the fight, one ship against over four dozen others, yet still refusing to back down.

It is hard to imagine what it must have been like on board that ship, knowing that there was no way out, yet the longer you carried on fighting the easier the fleet would be able to make distance. What is puzzling is why, out of fifty-three ships, did the Spanish not despatch just two-three to fight *Revenge* and send the rest after the English fleet? Perhaps they didn't want to split up the task force or maybe they simply didn't realise how close they had come to stumbling upon such a large number of ships. If they had have done that, we could have been looking at a major Spanish victory against the English instead of the other way round.

For the *Revenge* and Sir Richard Grenville, they have gone down in history as the bravest of the brave, now lost forever beneath the Atlantic.

One day off the island of Terceira in the Azores the wreck of the *Revenge* will be discovered, the stories will be retold and the artefacts from a long ago battle will be shown to those who love history. Until that day arrives the *Revenge* still sleeps beneath the waves, shrouded in the respect with which such a brave crew anointed it on that night in 1591.

Chapter 12

Bonhomme Richard

This next ship is not only one of the (if not the) most famous ships in American history but it is still missing despite press reports stating otherwise. It takes us back to the American War of Independence when Britain was fighting its colonies across the Atlantic as they campaigned to be a single nation with their own government. Although the famous Declaration of Independence was adopted on 4 July 1776, it was not signed that day, nor was independence granted until seven years later. By 1779 the French were involved on the side of the Americans and the *Duc de Duras*, a former trader, was sold to the Americans with a promise of later payment. She was renamed *Bonhomme Richard* by her captain, John Paul Jones. Ironically, Jones was from Scotland.

Born near Kirkbean in Dumfries and Galloway, he went to sea at a young age, but after many years of rising up the ranks he was involved in two deaths on board his ships that came under investigation. Not wanting to stick around and be hanged for what he claimed were accidents, he sailed away to join the fight on the opposite team. He even changed his name from John Paul to add on the Jones. At just 33 years old he was already responsible for sacking the western coastal town of Whitehaven in Cumbria and is one of three who earned the nickname 'Father of the American Navy'.

Sailing down the eastern coast of the British Isles in September 1779 with three other ships – *Alliance*, *Pallas* and *Vengeance* – they had visions of soon coming up against a British fleet and scoring a tremendous victory and it didn't take long before this was achieved as the fleet proceeded south off the Yorkshire coast. On 23 September the four ships sighted a British fleet of merchant ships with two warships for protection. The two ships HMSs *Serapis* and *Countess of Scarborough* stayed to fight in order to allow the convoy to escape. What followed next went down in history as the Battle of Flamborough Head.

That night, the ships fought each other at close quarters. People on the Head and the nearby town of Bridlington were lining the coast watching the explosions of the guns out at sea. On board the ships there was devastation, death and destruction but, when asked if he wanted to surrender, Jones is alleged to have shouted back 'I have not yet begun to fight!'

The *Serapis* and *Bonhomme Richard* ended up being joined together side by side as the guns carried on smashing each other up. During this phase of the fight the French ship *Vengeance* decided to circle the two ships and fired on both of them without worrying which one they were hitting. *Countess of Scarborough* was still putting up a fight but she was first to surrender.

Eventually the battered *Serapis* could take no more and surrendered to Jones. The crew were taken prisoner and the battle was over. This had gone on long into the night and now dozens of sailors were dead. *Bonhomme Richard* was in a very bad way and chances are that if Captain Richard Pearson of the *Serapis* had known just how bad, he might have stuck it out that little bit longer, but hindsight is a wonderful thing.

As the following day showed the true extent of the damage, as many things as possible were moved from *Bonhomme Richard* over to *Serapis* ready to sail to Holland, but they knew that the ship would not survive for much longer. Some sources claim as much as two days passed before finally the ship sank into the cold depths of the North Sea.

Jones returned a hero and would later become father of the Russian navy as the years went by. He died alone in a Paris apartment in 1792 aged just 45. The *Serapis* also sailed again and was burned and sunk in 1781 off Madagascar, its wreck being located in 1999. A final interesting point to this story was that Jones's body was missing until 1905 when he was located and identified after six years of searching. He was exhumed and brought to the US Naval Academy, Annapolis in Maryland where he is entombed today.

For the *Bonhomme Richard* the search for the wreck has occupied many people's thoughts and even today claims are still thrown around saying that it has been discovered. Clive Cussler once again reared his head in a number of searches, three in the late 1970s to early 1980s and one in 2004, but with no luck. He did, however, get a documentary made for his series 'The Sea Hunters' where he set sail with a team using a ship out of the fishing port of Whitby. Since then, the charter boat has been used several times over the years following the Cussler expeditions and using members of his team, but these were not publicised nor did they have any luck in finding the wreck.

Another historic wreck that is currently protected by the Protection of Wrecks Act 2002 lies in the middle of Filey Bay. It was discovered by John Adams and his dive team in 1974, announcing in 1998 that this could be *Bonhomme Richard*. While all signs point to it being of historical significance, it is highly unlikely to be Jones's ship due to the fact it is too close to land; it was far out to sea when she went down. This area does have several other wrecks from that era which could fit this site, but almost fifty years since it was discovered it seems identification of this wreck is no closer today than it was then.

Other claims have made the news over the years and it seems that people are so desperate to be the discoverer of this long-lost ship that any piece of driftwood that is found on the rocks is suddenly the *Bonhomme Richard*.

The closest anyone has come to finding her was by a number of expeditions led by the Ocean Technology Foundation. They first came to the area of the battle in 2006 and had a number of historians and experts with them to guide them towards likely targets. An initial survey of the seabed using sonar came up with some interesting results, some possible targets to look at later and some areas where there was nothing at all. Over the next few years, they returned a number of times and managed to locate a number of uncharted shipwrecks, some of them looking like promising targets. On one expedition, they brought along the world's smallest nuclear submarine *NR-1* which was borrowed with a crew from the US Navy. But, despite the professionalism and state of the art equipment used, the expeditions hit a dead end when there was a disagreement between France and the United States about ultimate ownership of the wreck – after all the Americans did not pay for the ship before she was sunk. With this kind of argument seemingly the priority of the sponsors it was inevitable that the project was suspended indefinitely.

The years once again tick by with no wreck found and it is a pity that a petty argument ended the most promising of the expeditions, but it is hoped that one day the world will once again gaze upon the remains of John Paul Jones's flagship, see her guns in a museum and tell the story once again. The wreck has eluded those who have the technology, expertise, knowledge and money, but each expedition has told us where the wreck of the *Bonhomme Richard* does not lie. Like it or not, this has still narrowed the search down.

Today there is a museum to Jones at his birthplace, a monument in Washington DC, a toposcope near the lighthouse at Flamborough Head and his tomb in Maryland. All we need now is a shipwreck hunter to do the final job of giving this story a satisfactory ending.

Chapter 13

USS *Cyclops*

There has never been a more serious loss of life on a shipwreck so mysterious as that of the US Navy coal collier *Cyclops*. To this day she remains the largest loss of life in the US Navy outside of combat and the fact that she simply disappeared has led to the usual conspiracy theories and is the top subject when it comes to talking about the Bermuda Triangle.

She was launched as an auxiliary to help fuel the fleet with coal, pretty much as the oil tankers of the modern navy do today, but the lack of ability to refuel the navy's warships was a potential weakness for them and so ships like the USS *Cyclops* were a godsend for a deployed unit. Launched in Philadelphia on 7 May 1910, she was 542 feet long and could carry over 12,000 tons of coal in her holds, although she did not commission until 1 May 1917, less than a month after America had joined the war on the side of the Entente against Imperial Germany.

At this time the navy's ships were going through a process of converting their fuel from coal to oil, so already time for the *Cyclops* was running out as progress was fast when it came to industry and engineering – many of the liners were already making that change. Her last journey started on 8 January 1918 when she was loaded with just under 10,000 tons of coal bound for Rio de Janeiro to assist with the British ships in that area, arriving there almost three weeks later and departing with a cargo of manganese ore on 15 February; she arrived in Bahia five days later.

On 22 February she set sail for Baltimore for the last leg of the journey home but went alongside in Barbados on 3 March, which was an unscheduled stop. She had previously reported engine trouble and had only been able to make around 10 knots. A survey team consulted with the captain and recommended she head back to the USA where repairs to a cracked cylinder could be carried out. At this point it was noticed that she may have been slightly overloaded with the extra coal she was bringing on board and may have had more cargo than planned when she had been sailing from Brazil. As the ship had only been operating for less than a year, she had not had any previous sailings carrying the ore.

With a plan in place, *Cyclops* set sail from Barbados on 4 March 1918 with a heavy cargo and 309 people in total. That was the last anybody ever saw of the ship or any of her crew.

Immediately it was thought she had been caught by a storm that had been seen in the Virginia Capes area. A passing ship said they may have seen her but nothing was confirmed. The sudden loss of the *Cyclops* and the lack of wreckage or distress calls led people to believe that whatever happened it had been quick.

The theories ranged from massive structural failure to her overloading causing her to sink quickly. Wilder conspiracies as usual reared their heads with the talk of supernatural forces causing the ship to vanish in the infamous Bermuda Triangle. Due to the area where she went down and the fact that so many previous ships had vanished without trace in that stretch of ocean it had now become the most famous place in the world for ships and aircraft to vanish and had gained a reputation as being the home of all sea mysteries.

Due to the First World War being such a huge event with ships sinking all the time, no investigation was launched into the loss of the *Cyclops*. Therefore, there was never a report into her loss. This again fuelled talk of a conspiracy, but it really wasn't as dark as what some people believed.

But one thing that has to be considered is that *Cyclops* was one of four sister ships of the Proteus-class colliers – *Jupiter*, *Proteus* and *Nereus* were the other three, all three of which would soon be at the bottom of the sea. *Jupiter* was converted to being an aircraft carrier and renamed the USS *Langley*, sinking during battle in 1942. But *Proteus* and *Nereus* were both lost in the same rough area as the *Cyclops* in 1941 with no trace of them ever being found. *Proteus* had fifty-eight crew lost at the time and *Nereus* had sixty-one.

With all three disappearances being put down to being in wartime, the obvious explanation was that a U-boat had targeted all three, but there is no evidence of this and a ship of this size would at least leave wreckage, survivors, a patch of fuel, or even be able to send one distress message. The fact that they were all lost in almost the same circumstances fuels the fire when trying to figure out the rational against unbelievable reasons behind the loss. While some experts believe that there was a fundamental flaw in this class of ship, the unmistakable fact that all three should suffer the same fate means that this cannot be ignored. But what was the difference between these and the fourth sister ship *Langley* (ex-*Jupiter*)? Being converted to an aircraft carrier involved radical and structurally different changes which could have prolonged any hull flaw. That she was no longer carrying vast quantities of heavy cargo meant that the stresses on the ship were so much different. Or she was just lucky not to have sunk in those circumstances. It does seem a huge coincidence either way.

The fact of the matter is that these three ships have vanished, their wrecks still lie at the bottom of the sea just waiting for somebody to come along, pinpoint them and bring the first images back. After 100 years it is highly unlikely that *Cyclops* will be sitting upright with the answer for all to see. Shipwrecks like this will slowly collapse over time and the reasons for their loss will be lost forever. With such a large area of ocean to search it is impossible to know where to start with a search. Had GPS technology existed, it could have at least narrowed down the area.

As it stands today, the USS *Cyclops* is the most talked about ship ever to vanish at sea and the worst non-combat disaster for the United States Navy. While she has been written about in books throughout the last century, nobody has come close to solving the mystery and, until the wreck is found and her exact location determined, it is likely that nobody ever will.

Chapter 14

HMS *Courageous*

Our journey now takes us to the era that is the Second World War, a six-year period when tens of thousands of sailors were killed in thousands of ships lost at sea. Some of the greatest vessels the world had ever seen would be destroyed by acts of inhumanity and terror. When the UK declared war on 3 September 1939 it did not take long before the first casualties were reported – indeed just eight hours later the liner *Athenia* was hit by a torpedo from a German U-boat and sank killing 117 people. The shock of this ship being struck within hours was felt across both sides of the Atlantic as it was revealed that Americans were on board and images of the *Lusitania* scandal twenty-four years before were at the forefront of people's minds.

For the Royal Navy, they had to be on high alert; the shock of some of the losses they had suffered when the *Aboukir*, *Hogue* and *Cressy* were sunk in just over an hour in 1914 was one they did not want to repeat. But, at the same time, these ships needed to be out and about patrolling the coastline, for it was only a matter of time before Hitler's troops set their sights on an invasion of the British Isles.

One of the ships on patrol was the aircraft carrier *Courageous*, a very special design considering she started life as a battle-cruiser. Built in Newcastle and launched in 1916, the ship was fitted with four 15-inch main guns as well as eighteen 4-inch guns in triple barbettes down each side. The ship looked like a modern dreadnought, 786 feet 9 inches long and a displacement of just over 19,000 tons, and one which would strike terror into the smaller ships. With so many vessels having been lost at the Battle of Jutland, the commissioning of *Courageous* was a welcome addition to the fleet.

After taking part in the Second Battle of Heligoland Bight in 1917 her role filtered down to almost nothing by the end of the war, remaining in Portsmouth as flagship and training ship for several years. But the Washington Treaty of 1922 forced the Royal Navy to think about its fleet after it was found that, although they could not build any new aircraft carriers, they could convert their existing ships and the hulls of ships like *Courageous* were perfect for such a role.

In 1924 the ship was taken to Devonport where her conversion began. She increased her weight to 24,000 tons and had her main decks stripped back and replaced with a flight deck around three quarters the length of her hull with a two-storey hangar underneath. An island was built on her starboard side as well as lifts to get the aircraft up onto the flight deck. By the time she had come out of refit in 1928 she looked a completely different ship. Her sister ship *Furious* had gone through the same treatment and already it seemed a perfect way to continue using these ships for what they needed, although *Furious* wasn't built with an island; instead she had a flat deck to work from.

Able to carry up to forty-eight aircraft, she conducted trials off the south coast near the Isle of Wight and, from May 1928, was assigned to the Mediterranean fleet. At the outbreak of war, she was already back with the Home Fleet and had sailed from Devonport that day with a destroyer escort. She was patrolling the south-western coast under the command of Captain Makeig-Jones in the hunt for the deadly German U-boats and on 17 September 1939 was over 300 miles from Land's End with her escort ships when they picked up and responded to a distress call from a cargo ship that had been attacked. Swordfish aircraft were launched which went in to attack the U-boat, but nearby was another submarine lying in wait. The aircraft landed back on board and the ship prepared them for another sortie.

U-29 was watching the aircraft carrier squadron with interest. Through the periscope, 30-year-old *Kapitänleutnant* Otto Schuhart could see the carrier turn into the wind to conduct the next flying serial, now that the previous squadron had returned. With the ship lined up in his sights he gave the order to fire three torpedoes. Seconds later they were heading towards *Courageous*. Two of the torpedoes found their target as they blasted into her port side which caused chaos straightaway with a loss of power. Water flooded into the holes and sailors scrambled to get out from down below. Within minutes, it was clear that *Courageous* was doomed and the aim now was to get over 1,200 people off the ship as quickly as possible. The carrier was listing heavily as the lower compartments were lost one by one. Already the ships in the area were torn between hunting the submarine and helping the ship in distress.

It didn't take long for a ship of this size to disappear beneath the waves. In less than twenty minutes *Courageous* had listed over and capsized taking over 500 of her crew with her to the seabed. The sea was now littered with sailors who, just half an hour before, had not known that this would be their predicament, treading water in the swells of the cold Atlantic waiting for the escort ships to pick them up. A flurry of activity ensued and, slowly but surely, the survivors were plucked from the sea and taken on board. Several more died in the coming days, taking the eventual deal toll to 519 including the captain.

The escort destroyer HMS *Impulsive* made an attempt to chase down the U-boat with depth charges but had no luck and the *U-29* escaped to fight another day. Upon their return to Germany the captain was awarded the Iron Cross First Class and the entire crew of the submarine given the Iron Cross Second Class, such was the German jubilation over the sinking of the first British warship to be sunk in combat during the Second World War.

The legacy of this attack and an unsuccessful attempt to sink HMS *Ark Royal* just days earlier led to aircraft carriers being withdrawn from these patrols.

The story of HMS *Courageous* is well known, yet so little is written about her life and loss. There are no big screen movies or great shipwreck searches for this ship, yet her transformation from a battle-cruiser to an aircraft carrier only for her to be lost to be less than twenty minutes after a double torpedo strike shows just how quickly the tide could turn on a warship during the Second World War. While some websites claim that the wreck has been located, there is no information on its condition. What is more likely is that the last reported position has been noted and taken as being where the remains of *Courageous* lie today. With recent Pacific aircraft-carrier discoveries making the headlines in the last ten years it would be a fitting end to her story to have the images of this amazing ship broadcast to the world once again.

Chapter 15

HMS *Glorious*

F*urious* and *Courageous* were not the only ships to be converted from a regular heavy-gun surface ships to aircraft carriers. While these two had many differences, *Glorious* was the third of the Courageous-class sister ships and had more in common with *Courageous* when it came to her design and build.

Like her sister in the previous chapter, *Glorious* had been launched as a battle-cruiser from the Harland and Wolff shipyard in Belfast on 20 April 1916 and commissioned in the January of the following year. Taking part in the Second Battle of Heligoland Bight on 17 November 1917 she suffered several hits and damage to her turret following a premature detonation of her own ammunition.

On 5 November 1918, just a few days before the end of the First World War, she was at anchor in the Firth of Forth with the seaplane-tender *Campania* and battleship *Royal Oak* when a change in the weather caused *Campania* to drag her anchor and collide with both ships. Although *Glorious* and *Royal Oak* only sustained a minimal amount of damage, *Campania* eventually sank following flooding caused by the collision.

After the war *Glorious* was there when the German High Seas Fleet surrendered and from then on she was used as a training ship in Devonport, as her sister was doing in Portsmouth. With the Washington Treaty, the three sisters were converted to aircraft carriers, *Glorious* going into the docks in 1924 and not returning to sea until 1930 when she was ready for sea trials.

Like *Courageous* she had an island on the starboard side of the flight deck and the deck went around three-quarters of her length, more than enough room to take off. When placed next to each other *Courageous* and *Glorious* were almost identical; it was the significant shape of the bows that told them apart from a distance.

Heading out to the Mediterranean in June 1930 to relieve *Courageous*, she was involved in a collision with the French ocean liner *Florida* on 1 April 1931, which caused severe damage to the carrier's bow, killed one member of her crew and forced her to head to Gibraltar for repairs. The liner suffered twenty-four dead and major damage to her port side in front of the bridge.

When war broke out *Glorious* was still in the Med and briefly went through to the Indian Ocean via the Suez Canal to hunt for the German raider *Admiral Graf Spee* and then returned to her station later. In April 1940, she was brought back to home waters to take part in the campaign to prevent Norway being taken over by the Germans.

She was heavily involved in flying operations around the Narvik area and even had a squadron of Hurricanes take off from her deck, and come back again, amongst other aircraft. Things were going well but the action was fast paced, with the fleet having the constant threat of attack. Her commanding officer was Captain Guy D'Oyly-Hughes, a highly-decorated submariner but also a man who was not popular with his crew and extremely harsh to his officers. On one occasion it was reported that he placed a gun on the bridge in case anybody wanted to think about disobeying his orders. Ruling a ship using fear was not a good idea and so, on more than one occasion, he clashed with members of his ship's company. His Commander (Air) had been taken off ship for refusing to carry out an order to bomb targets that he could not achieve due to the aircraft and the targets themselves not being properly defined. He had permission to proceed to Scapa Flow to attend the court martial and so *Glorious* turned for Scotland under escort from the destroyers *Acasta* and *Ardent*.

On the afternoon of 8 June 1940, the German battleships *Scharnhorst* and *Gneisenau* sighted the fleet and opened fire, hitting the *Ardent* and causing her to flee under a smoke screen. Several more hits on the ship stopped her dead in the water and she sank soon after. In the meantime, they had also found their target in *Glorious* and the flight deck took a direct strike which started fires in the hangar, rendering the ship useless as an aircraft carrier.

The two German ships pounded *Glorious* again and the crippled carrier lost speed and started to flood, listing heavily to starboard. Just over two hours after first being sighted, the *Glorious* went down.

Now the two battleships turned their attention to the last of the two destroyers, *Acasta*, who had been trying to lay smoke screens to protect the carrier, but time was running out for it. A destroyer against two heavily-armed German battleships that had already sunk the other two had no chance. But *Acasta* still put up a fight and scored several hits on *Scharnhorst*, but inevitably she was never going to win. *Acasta* went down at 1820.

In less than three hours the ships were gone. The Germans fled quickly, thinking that a fleet of ships would be coming to the aid of *Glorious* and the escorts and this would have included air cover. But, in fact, there were no rescue ships inbound. The first the British knew of the loss was when it was heard over German radio. Only two days later did rescue ships begin to search for survivors. Of the three ships, there was one survivor from each destroyer and just thirty-eight from *Glorious*. A total of 1,519 people had died on the three ships, 1,207 from *Glorious* alone.

The loss was a devastating blow to the Narvik campaign, as well as to the Royal Navy in general. The controversy over the lack of knowledge of the sinking was felt within the ranks when it was thought that a nearby ship in radio silence had known about it but couldn't take action. Such is the tragedy of wartime sinkings such as this that there are always questions that are followed by answers that are painful to digest.

Today there are several memorials to the crews of the three ships, the organisation GLARAC (*Glorious Ardent Acasta* Association) being instrumental in ensuring that the memory of these three ships and the crews who served on them are never forgotten. An excellent book by John Winton named *Carrier Glorious* goes into detail about the ship's career, final voyage and controversy surrounding the problems with the captain. It is one of the most in-depth accounts of the life of this incredible ship that had such a busy career and did so much for the war effort spanning thousands of miles.

Like her sister ship *Courageous*, sunk less than a year before, her wreck remains lost along with those of her escorts *Acasta* and *Ardent*.

Chapter 16

HMS *Barham*

The Second World War was a conflict that ripped the world apart in many ways. The war at sea saw some of the most horrendous fighting imaginable and led to many families at home receiving telegrams announcing that a sailor had been killed, wounded or was missing in action. Very few of these sea fights or incidents were caught on camera, but the demise of the battleship HMS *Barham* was an exception and is one of the most shocking pieces of footage from the war.

Barham was a Queen Elizabeth-class battleship, one of five that were commissioned for the Royal Navy during the First World War period. She was completed and sent to sea in 1915. At 643 feet and 9 inches long with a displacement of around 33,000 tons, *Barham* boasted four 15-inch guns in two large turrets facing forward, as well as a variety of smaller weapons. At the time she was one of the most modern and deadly battleships in the fleet.

She was joining the fleet at a very volatile time. the Battle of Jutland on 31 May 1916 saw her steaming east to meet the German fleet for one of the most explosive and devastating battles in history. Joining Admiral Beatty's squadron, she headed out and went to action that afternoon targeting the Grand Fleet which had come out of Germany to battle with their formidable enemy.

Barham saw continuous action in the battle and was hit by several shells from the *Derfflinger* that caused holes to appear in her hull and superstructure. By the end of the battle the ship had a total of twenty-six killed and twenty-six injured personnel. She journeyed back to port for repairs (a section of her hull with a shell hole is today on display at the Imperial War Museum and has featured in the centenary of Jutland exhibition in Portsmouth).

In between the wars *Barham* was mostly stationed in the Mediterranean but on the outbreak of war it was decided to bring her back to Britain and have her as part of the Home Fleet. In December 1939 she was being escorted by four destroyers back to the River Clyde when, on 12 December, she accidentally rammed the destroyer HMS *Duchess* in the night. The ship was just nine miles from the Mull of Kintyre, so close to home, 136 people on board being killed as the destroyer turned upside down and sank in the inky blackness. There were just twenty-four survivors rescued (See *Collision in the Night: The sinking of HMS* Duchess, also written by the author).

Barham arrived in the Clyde that same day and within days was back at sea. On 28 December she was hit by a torpedo from a nearby U-boat and four crewmen were killed, but the ship survived and went to Birkenhead for repairs.

Heading back to the Mediterranean the year after, she was involved in the Battle of Dakar in the unsuccessful attempt to deny the port to the Germans.

It was in March 1941 that *Barham* found herself taking part in the Battle of Cape Matapan, along with several other ships that included the battleships *Valiant* and *Warspite*.. On board *Valiant* was Philip Mountbatten, Prince Philip of Greece and Denmark, who would marry HRH Princess Elizabeth and become Duke of Edinburgh. The aircraft carrier *Formidable* sent up aircraft to attack the Italian fleet which, although putting up quite a fight, lost five warships and 2,300 killed compared to Allied losses of three killed and a few ships damaged.

By November 1941 *Barham* had seen a fair amount of action in the Med, but her time was coming to an end. Sailing from Alexandria to hunt for Italian convoys, *Barham*, *Valiant* and *Queen Elizabeth* were escorted out to sea by eight destroyers. On 25 November *U-331* located the fleet and lined one of the ships up for a torpedo attack. But the sub was detected by a destroyer and chased away, although not before her captain, *Oberleutnant zur See* Hans-Diedrich von Tiesenhausen, ordered four torpedoes away. He did not see the result of the attack but believed he had hit one of the battleships. He was right.

Three of the torpedoes slammed into *Barham* amidships at close proximity to each other. Immediately, the ship took on a severe list to port. HMS *Valiant* was nearby and on board was a cameraman from Pathé News who started filming what was happening. The ship was listing over so far that the crew of *Barham* were running down the hull itself and sliding off the bottom of the ship, the size of the ship making the fleeing crew look like an army of ants running out of their nest.

Then suddenly *Barham*'s magazine exploded, a huge explosion ripping the vessel up with huge chunks of the ship flying in every direction as the smoke, dust and wreckage shot skywards. Those watching from the side-lines could hardly believe what they were seeing. Within seconds the huge battleship had gone.

Of the ship's company, 862 were lost, the 450 survivors being picked up by the ships around her. A sea of bodies and wreckage littered the area where *Barham* had been.

The news of the *Barham* sinking was not made public, but letters of condolence were sent out to the families of those who died and this triggered a rather bizarre episode of the British legal system when a woman named Helen Duncan held a séance at the ship's home port of Portsmouth. Duncan was a medium who claimed to have contact with the spirit world but had been found out on several occasions making fraudulent claims. But at this meeting she announced that she had reached the spirit of a sailor from HMS *Barham* who told her that the ship had been sunk. Because this had only been told to the relatives and not announced in the newspapers, the Royal Navy took an interest in what was going on. She was arrested and put on trial under the Witchcraft Act of 1735, which covered fraudulent activity, and it caused quite a stir when she was in court. She was found guilty on one charge and sent to prison for nine months, the last witch trial in the United Kingdom. There are still people in Britain today who believe she should be pardoned.

The loss of *Barham* was a tragic chapter in the Royal Navy's Mediterranean campaign. The ship had achieved so much in her twenty-five-year life and had suffered a painful ending, not least highlighted by the witch trial which even Winston Churchill called a misuse of court resources.

There are several memorials to the lost of the *Barham*. Their names are on the Portsmouth Naval Memorial, along with several smaller tributes underneath. The National Memorial Arboretum has a granite tribute, along with a bench to the left of it paying respect to all those who served on *Barham* from the launch in 1914 to her sinking in 1941.

Today the wreck of the *Barham* is at the bottom of the Mediterranean. She has never been located but we can only imagine what condition she is in following such a devastating explosion that sent her to the bottom so quickly.

Chapter 17

HMS *Kelly*

One of the most famous names in modern Royal Naval history is that of the *Kelly*, but it is not necessarily the ship itself that is famous, more her captain, because this ship was not only led by a famous name, but a name with links to the Royal Family.

Named after the former Admiral of the Fleet Sir John Kelly, she was launched on 25 October 1938, too late for the Admiral to see his ship as he had died at the age of 65 just two years before. A K-class destroyer, *Kelly* was one of eight of her class and built in Tyne and Wear. Commissioning in August 1939, just in time to see the start of the Second World War, at 356.5 feet long, she displaced 2,400 tons fully loaded and was armed with six 4.7-inch guns in three turrets, as well as various anti-aircraft weapons and torpedo tubes.

Her captain was Lord Louis Mountbatten, also previously known as Prince Louis of Battenberg, second cousin to King George VI and a Royal Navy officer. Joining the Navy in 1916, he was promoted to captain just ten days before the declaration of war with Germany and became commanding officer of the *Kelly* straight out of build. He also commanded the 5th Destroyer Flotilla from his new ship. On 12 September his first mission was to collect a VIP and his wife from France – the former King Edward VIII and Wallis Simpson, by then known as the Duke and Duchess of Windsor. *Kelly* took them back from le Havre and brought them into Portsmouth.

Towards the wintertime *Kelly* had to be sent for repairs in dry dock after storm damage had caused the ship a month's worth of work, but she was soon back at sea again. However, the ship didn't last until the end of the year before sustaining her first damage from the war, when a tanker struck a mine on 14 December 1939 and *Kelly* was sent along with three rescue tugs and the destroyer HMS *Mohawk* to assist. During the rescue operation *Kelly* struck a mine herself and had to be towed up the Tyne for repairs that saw her back in the docks for the next few months.

Incredibly, her run of bad luck continued when, just two days after returning to sea, she was in collision with the destroyer HMS *Gurkha* which had her back in dry dock for another two months, this time on the Thames. She would eventually be back at sea at the end of April 1940, having had more time in dry dock than as a warship at sea.

Kelly was sent to assist in the Norwegian campaign and headed towards yet more danger as the night of 9 May 1940 saw British and German forces clash at sea into the following morning. *Kelly* was torpedoed by a German E-boat and the damage was so bad the ship looked as if she was sinking. But a tug took her in tow and very slowly made their way back to Britain. On top of the obvious damage to the ship, twenty-seven of her crew had lost their lives, but the ordeal was not over. During the next four days *Kelly* and the towing ship (as they got close to land, the tug *Great Emperor*) came under attack from both aircraft and E-boats and yet still she would not succumb to the enemy's fire, even when she was rammed by an enemy vessel. Incredibly the ship made it to the Tyne where she was put straight into dry dock and her damage inspected. Photographs of the *Kelly* entering the river show just how close the ship came to the water overlapping her upper decks. She was brought home by the excellent training in damage control and a very large bit of good luck for it is likely that any rough weather would have finished her off.

It would be another seven months in dry dock for *Kelly* before she was able to get back out to sea. She had taken more damage in her time than any other ship and just kept coming back. Out of her entire time in commission, she had been at sea for less than two weeks.

By April 1941 it was decided that the *Kelly* would be sent to the Mediterranean and sailed from Plymouth to join Force S to reinforce the fleet there. This was a crucial time for the Med as British convoys were coming under constant attack and the Italian convoys needed to be stopped; all the while the countries around them were falling to Nazi Germany one by one. On 22 May she was sent to Crete with HMS *Kashmir* and HMS *Kipling* to help defend the island and prevent any invading forces from making landfall. But it was not going to be an easy fight.

The following day the ships came under attack near the island. German dive bombers spotted them as they were heading to intercept suspect fishing vessels that were thought to be carrying German reinforcements. A 1,000lb bomb was dropped on the *Kashmir* which was ripped apart in seconds, but not before 28-year-old Ian Rhodes, one of *Kashmir*'s gunners, shot down the offending aircraft. Incredibly he survived and for his actions was later awarded the Conspicuous Gallantry Medal (second only to the

Victoria Cross), but now the attention of the aircraft was focused on the next ship – HMS *Kelly*.

As with *Kashmir*, a bomb made a direct hit on the aft X-turret and smashed through to just aft of the engine room before detonating. Within two minutes, the ship had flooded and capsized, her surviving crew jumping overboard for their lives to join the sea of faces already being rescued from *Kashmir*. The *Kelly* finally sank while the aircraft were still gunning survivors in the water.

The final death toll for both ships was eighty for *Kashmir* and another 130 dead in *Kelly*. In Hebburn Cemetery a memorial was created for the crew of the *Kelly*, honouring not only those who died off Crete but also the twenty-seven others who were lost off Norway.

The loss of HMS *Kelly* would have most likely been no more significant than any other ship lost in the war, but Lord Mountbatten being her captain changed that. He later became Admiral of the Fleet and the last Viceroy of India while his connections with the Royal Family went further as his nephew became the Duke of Edinburgh when he married Princess Elizabeth in 1947. He continued to have both naval and political influence for many years right up until his murder by the IRA in a boat bombing in August 1979.

For the *Kelly*, although her wreck has not been located, she is remembered in various ways. A group known as the HMS *Kelly* Association keeps her memory alive and has been known to host many memorial services and remembrance events to make sure that the name of *Kelly* lives on.

Chapter 18

USS *Oklahoma*

The date of 7 December 1941 will forever be known in American history as 'A date which will live in infamy'. For this date is when the Second World War changed dramatically in the sudden Japanese attack on the US Naval base at Pearl Harbor, Hawaii. Before this date the United States had been neutral, reluctant to enter the war against Germany but still assisting the Allies with the sale of hardware to help with the war effort. But during this time tensions were rising on the other side of the world with Japan and it was only a matter of time before the touch-paper was lit. In this case Japan decided to strike first. A huge fleet was put together and low-level bombing raids were practised ready for a surprise attack on the American fleet which would be at anchor in Pearl Harbor. It was hoped that they would sink an entire fleet of battleships and aircraft carriers in three waves of air attacks. The training completed, the fleet set sail in radio silence to their target at Oahu, Hawaii.

The base had been used for the Pacific Fleet since 1899 and had grown to be the main Pacific operating station with dry docks, aircraft hangars, airfields and port facilities. One of the ships anchored at Battleship Row on the morning of the attack was the USS *Oklahoma*.

The *Oklahoma* was by now an old battleship, being launched in March 1914 and was coming up to 28 years old. At 583 feet long and just over 27,000 tons, she had a crew complement of almost 1,400. Her armament consisted of two triple and two twin 14-inch guns as well as the usual anti-aircraft guns and torpedo tubes and a catapult for launching her two aircraft that she carried on board.

Not doing much in the First World War other than escort duties and patrols, she spent the next two decades taking part in exercises and training serials with other ships, although she was involved in the evacuation of American citizens when the Spanish Civil War broke out in 1936.

After much thought and with her being used more for training as time went on, it was decided that the *Oklahoma* would be retired in May 1942.

But on 7 December 1941 the early Sunday morning peace was shattered by explosions coming from the dockyard. The Pearl Harbor attack had begun while the sailors were still sleeping or planning a lazy routine. Within minutes, fires and explosions were rocking the ships at anchor.

The *Oklahoma* was berthed outboard alongside the *Maryland* when, suddenly, two torpedoes slammed into her side. Although the hull wasn't penetrated it still caused considerable damage. The crew raced to their positions and tried to use the anti-aircraft guns but the firing locks were in the armoury and so couldn't be used. A third torpedo penetrated the hull and, this time, water began flooding into the ship at a vast rate. It was still only 0800 hours.

Oklahoma started taking on a severe list straightaway, her crew now not only fighting the Japanese aircraft but fighting to survive. More torpedoes slammed into the hull as the list grew worse. As many as nine torpedoes struck the devastated ship as bombs and torpedoes rained down on the other ships nearby. At 0806 the nearby battleship USS *Arizona* took a direct bomb hit and exploded in a huge blast that killed most of her crew instantly, smoke and debris shooting off high into the air. This one ship alone accounted for a vast amount of the casualties that day.

In the meantime, the stricken *Oklahoma* was beyond saving. The list was so severe that she was almost on her side. In just a few minutes the ship had been devastated and the crew scrambled to get off to safety. For many they wouldn't make it as the battleship rolled onto her side and carried on going, her superstructure crushed on the seabed as the weight of the hull filling with water led to the ship only settling once it had rolled over by 135 degrees.

For many there was no escape, only a few lucky ones being able to get out of the steel tomb. Banging was heard on the hull but eventually even that died out. The whole event had lasted approximately twelve minutes from the first torpedo strike. Of her full complement of crew, only thirty-two people were dragged out of the upturned wreck that hadn't already escaped; 429 others were killed.

Following the surprise attack on Pearl Harbor, the United States of America declared war on Japan. President Roosevelt made his 'date of infamy' speech and the world was now changing once again. For Pearl Harbor itself, there were no aircraft carriers there that day and so the third wave of aircraft were called off, the damage to the battleships severe enough. The *Arizona* had lost 1,177 people, *Oklahoma* 429; the total for the day was a shocking 2,403 killed and 1,178 injured.

For now, the harbour was a complete wreck and salvage plans had to start immediately. The battleships USS *Arizona* and USS *Utah* would remain in situ as a memorial to what happened. For the *Oklahoma* and the rest of the ships sunk, they would be salvaged and, if possible, put back into service, although as *Oklahoma* was due to be retired anyway it was always highly unlikely that she would re-enter service.

But, after much delay, it was not until 8 March 1943 that the first attempts began to right the upturned hull. Twenty-one winches were rigged on land close to the ship, each with cables fixed to the hull to work in pulling very slowly until the ship was upright again. This lasted until June when they could finally say that the ship was now on an even keel once more, eighteen months after she had rolled over.

Salvage teams then had the job of removing the dead as well as all the pollutants within, such as fuel and toxic gas. The bodies of the crew were still being found in June 1944. Eventually, the ship was decommissioned and declared a derelict, remaining in Pearl Harbor for several years until finally it was decided to send her to the scrapyard. By then she was nothing more than a hull, all her superstructure and guns taken away and barely resembling the proud ship she once was.

In 1946 she was purchased by a company in California who despatched two tugs named *Hercules* and *Monarch* to tow her to San Francisco. She departed Pearl Harbor for the final time in May 1947 and headed towards mainland America.

On 17 May the ships entered an area of rough weather, the storm getting worse as the journey went on. They had made a journey so far of around 500 miles and there were dignitaries waiting in California to say a final farewell to the ship, but *Oklahoma* was never going to make it. The hulk of the battleship began taking on water once again, listing heavily in the stormy seas.

Oklahoma was going down fast and the speed of it almost took the two tugs down with her, but there was nothing that could be done. She went under for the last time still attached to the *Hercules* which only just managed to break free from the sinking ship.

In 2015 it was announced that efforts were being made to identify a number of unknown victims buried after the attack. Within four years they had identified, by DNA testing, 343 members of the ship's company of the USS *Oklahoma*; fifty-one others were returned to their resting place unidentified.

Today the wreck of *Oklahoma* lies at the bottom of the Pacific. As most were salvaged and put back into service and the *Arizona* and *Utah* left where they are as memorials, the only wreck from Pearl Harbor still undiscovered is the hulk of what was once the battleship *Oklahoma*.

Chapter 19

F4

The story of the Falklands War in 1982 has been well documented in the last forty years. The loss of life in such a short space of time was shocking, as was the loss of so many ships. The islands were invaded by Argentina on 2 April 1982 after the island of South Georgia had been overrun days before. British Prime minister Margaret Thatcher was determined to get the islands back and so a fleet of over 100 ships was ordered to sail with thousands of troops on board. One of the ships was HMS *Fearless*.

Fearless was launched in 1963 from the Harland and Wolff shipyard in Belfast, a new design of amphibious warship known as a LPD (Landing Platform Dock). In a revolutionary new way of conducting this kind of warfare, the ship was designed to flood her aft ballast tanks until low enough in the water for a huge door to open. With an internal docking area flooded, four large landing craft known as LCUs (Landing Craft Utility – numbers *F1* to *F4*) could be powered up and driven out, loaded with personnel, vehicles, stores and weapons. *Fearless* carried four of these in her dock as well as four smaller ones launched from the ship's side on davits; those were LCVPs (Landing Craft Vehicle and Personnel, numbered *F5* to *F8*). Together with her sister ship, *Intrepid*, the two vessels would be the backbone of the landings when it came to retaking the Falklands.

The LCUs were durable workhorses of the assault squadrons, a stern wheelhouse giving a full view of what was in the main bay, a large drop-down door at the bow so the vessel could just run up onto a beach and the troops pour out as they did on D Day for Operation OVERLORD in in Normandy in June 1944. At 240 tons displacement, these craft were almost 98 feet in length and powered by two diesel engines. They could carry up to four vehicles or over 100 personnel, their crews permanently assigned to a craft in order to maintain and operate when required.

At the beginning of May the fleet was already off the islands and a torpedo from a submarine sank the cruiser *General Belgrano* an incident that caused the Argentines to keep their navy away from the conflict. By

the end of May, the British had lost several key vessels to air attacks –
two destroyers and two frigates, as well as a civilian cargo ship being used
for supplies. As May turned into June the fighting intensified and the
Argentine army was being pushed back.

Tuesday 8 June 1982 is one of those dates that will always be remembered
for the events of the day, when Argentine aircraft bombed the LSLs
(Landing Ships Logistics) the RFA *Sir Galahad* and RFA *Sir Tristram*
with heavy loss of life, but few realised that a third vessel had been hit
earlier in the day – one of the landing craft from *Fearless* named *Foxtrot 4*.

The man in charge of *F4*, Colour Sergeant Brian Johnston, had risked
both his vessel and crew to try to get as many survivors off the sinking
frigate HMS *Antelope* just two weeks ago. That had earned the crew of *F4*
a huge amount of respect and would later lead to Johnston being awarded
the Queen's Gallantry Medal for the rescue. Considering that there was an
unexploded bomb just waiting to detonate in the bowels of *Antelope*, the
crew didn't complain once. This was an action that was never forgotten by
the crew of the frigate who are still grateful for *F4*'s actions even today.

On 8 June a group of personnel from the army needed a lift with all
their equipment across the water from Goose Green and *F4* navigated all
the way down Choiseul Sound in the dark and picked them up. Turning
around and heading back the way they came, on board were eight crew of
F4 and nine members of the British army. In full daylight and at constant
risk of attack the vessel made its way back.

At 1400 hours the first wave of enemy aircraft attacked the two LSLs,
causing major damage and many deaths. Two hours later, while *F4* was still
halfway down the Sound, another wave of aircraft came in to attack. At
around 1650 hours, *F4* was the target.

A bomb was dropped and scored a direct hit on the landing craft's
wheelhouse and stern area, the blast killing six people straight away and
crippling the small vessel. A nearby cargo ship, *Monsunnen*, came to
the rescue and manoeuvred into position to give *F4* a tow, the survivors
being taken off in the meantime. Although all the army personnel were
accounted for, only two of *F4*'s crew had survived. The dead included
Colour Sergeant Johnston.

Monsunnen began to make headway but it was not to be for *F4* as water
was flooding the inner compartments and she was sinking. Eventually, the
tow was released and *F4* slipped beneath the waves of Choiseul Sound.
The survivors were landed and eventually flown back to Britain, but the

front pages of the next day's papers concentrated on the devastation that was the large death toll on *Sir Galahad*, with forty-eight dead and a huge fire blazing on board, *Sir Tristram* had two dead and damage that could be repaired. The sinking of *F4* was a brief mention in some of the papers as 'a landing craft' had sunk and that is it. The loss of her six crew was not even a footnote in the newspapers.

On 14 June 1982, just six days after the loss of *F4*, victory was declared when the Argentine forces surrendered. The conflict had cost the lives of 255 British, 649 Argentines and three locals, as well as over a dozen ships and smaller vessels that now littered the seabed around the islands.

As with any war there are memorials and *F4* was not forgotten in that way. A monument was built on the coast near to where the craft was thought to have gone down. On board HMS *Fearless*, they mourned the loss of their shipmates with a yearly memorial service and two plaques placed on board – one in the Junior Rates' Dining Hall and a second outside the Commanding Officer's cabin. The replacement landing craft was not renamed *F4* but instead *FJ*, in honour of *F4*'s coxswain, Brian Johnston. Although *Fearless* was decommissioned in 2002, her and *Intrepid*'s replacement vessels *Albion* and *Bulwark* today carry on that tradition with a yearly ceremony and a craft numbered *FJ*.

With the other ships that went down, they had all the publicity and coverage. The image of HMS *Antelope* exploding was caught on camera, the burning HMS *Sheffield* or the capsizing HMS *Coventry* all making front pages. But *F4* was never given much publicity and only today is the story of this craft finally being told in news articles and blogs. The internet has biographies of each of the 255 British personnel who died on various websites so the six who died can be looked up without a problem. The story of what happened is slowly but surely coming to light and, as I did research for a book I was going to write on the craft, it was evident that there were a lot of people hoping that the wreck would be located.

Situated in relatively shallow waters, *F4* should be in one piece and easily located, but several searches by the Royal Navy in that area over the last few decades have not found any trace of this vessel. It could be the seabed disguising her when search teams run the sonar over or it could just be that she is not where the rescuers thought she was. Out of all the shipwrecks covered in this book, *F4* is most likely going to be found one day, hopefully sooner rather than later so that the families of those killed and the survivors still suffering with traumatic memories of that day can finally lay some ghosts to rest.

Until then, we wait and see and hope that another expedition is soon forthcoming.

Part III
Submarines

Chapter 20

Turtle

As we progress through the ages in maritime history the weaponry gets more accurate, the vehicles faster and the ships get more modern, but nowhere did a design have as much controversy as that of the first submarines. When they were introduced as a serious design of a vessel in the late 1800s/early 1900s, they were seen as 'damn Un-English' as one comment was heard. But the first ever submarines were so experimental that each dive was a risk to life and to carry out a real life mission was so doomed to fail that it would be a wonder that anybody would even risk it.

But risk it they did and in the 1600s the *Drebbel* became the first submarine to submerge and carry a crew in the River Thames, although going any further with a design was still a long, long way off. By the American War of Independence (1776-1783) there was a period of time where innovation seemed to be key to the fight and David Bushnell came up with a unique underwater contraption that he christened *Turtle*.

Nothing more than a farmer, Bushnell had an idea that was completely out of the ordinary, studying at Yale until he could turn his idea into a reality. He experimented with various ways of making a submarine that could deliver an attack by attaching explosive devices to the underside of a ship without it knowing the submarine was there. Together with his brother Ezra, Bushnell began constructing the *Turtle*.

He wanted to make sure that this was not just a usual diving bell attached to a support ship on the surface by tubes and ropes, but a free vehicle that was able to propel itself by a system of mechanisms and a propeller to allow it to move around when submerged. By 1776 the *Turtle* had been completed and the brothers got to work on perfecting their sub and to allow it to do the job for which they had designed it.

What they had built did look like two turtle shells clamped together (hence the name), made of oak and resembling some kind of spherical ale barrel. Valves were added to allow the pilot to stabilise the sub and to flood the tanks in order to ascend and descend as required. The size of it was only just big enough to fit a man inside, although cramped and with no room to stand up straight. The small viewing port at the very top was the only way the crewman could know which way he was going as the craft was surfaced. But the way this vessel was designed to attack another ship was as primitive as it got.

This would involve a mine, basically a device filled with gunpowder, which would be attached to the underside of an enemy ship using a screw that was operated from inside the sub. The screw would slowly drill into the wooden hull and then the sub would back off and leave the charge hanging from the screw while it made its escape.

The brothers moved the submarine once it had been finalised to the Connecticut river where they conducted tests and trained the operator in how it worked. It turned out that Ezra was the better operator as it required a lot of physical strength and he was built a lot better for this than David. Word spread amongst the American people and the hierarchy began taking an interest in the *Turtle*, so much so that they kept a close eye on the project as it progressed and eventually moved over to New York.

In June 1776 a fleet of British ships anchored in New York harbour with troops and supplies and this was seen as an excellent opportunity to strike the British when they least expected it. The flagship of Admiral Howe was HMS *Eagle* which became the primary target, although Ezra became ill in the meantime and was replaced by a volunteer named Ezra Lee. He was trained in the operation of the sub and how to plant the device and, a few weeks later, the mission was given a go ahead.

On 6 September 1776 the *Turtle* set out for the *Eagle* which was at anchor off Governor's Island, it was late at night and the aim was to blow the ship up under cover of darkness. But the tides were making his journey exhausting and he spent several hours fighting against the tides trying to make headway towards the ship.

By the time he got to the stern of *Eagle* the sun was coming up and people were already on deck. Close enough to even hear them speak, he closed his doors and submerged under the bottom of the ship. As he tried to screw the mine to the hull he was failing and time was not on his side. With the threat of discovery ever more present he abandoned his mission and headed back to shore. Nearby boats saw his craft and gave chase, but he set the mine off in the middle of the harbour and that scared them away enough for him to make his escape.

There were several more attempts to use *Turtle* to blow British ships up but they too failed when the sub was spotted, the current and tides again not giving them a fighting chance to achieve their mission.

It was a few days later that a British attack on ships in the area led to the vessel carrying *Turtle* being sunk on the Hudson river. Although there were rumours of it being salvaged, its fate is unknown. *Turtle* went down in history as the first ever submersible craft ever to attack another ship. Even though it was unsuccessful, it made the pages of the history books and was the forerunner of subsequent submarine designs.

The name *Turtle* and the design itself is today famous, replicas springing up all over the world in maritime museums and science displays, but where the sub is today could be anyone's guess. But you can bet that if it was discovered it would be proudly placed on display as a small boat that helped shape the history of maritime warfare.

Chapter 21
X5

The Second World War saw many people conduct themselves in such a way that the highest honours were merited; others went down in history for incredible feats of bravery, strength, leadership and devotion to their country. One such example is the crew who took part in Operation SOURCE, an attack on a German battleship that was so daring that it seemed that there was no way it would succeed. But succeed it did.

The Royal Navy had already seen what the *Bismarck* could do in just two weeks in 1941, which is why so much of the fleet deployed in the Atlantic to chase her down and sink her. But *Bismarck* was one of two sisters and the *Tirpitz* was going to be just as deadly if she wasn't stopped from breaking out and attacking the convoys.

Launched in April 1939 and ready for sea at the beginning of 1941, she was a beast of a ship – 823.5 feet long and displacing 52,000 tons, armed with eight 15-inch guns on four turrets and packed with many other weapons of war that made this fighting machine one of the largest in the world. It was the aim of the British to prevent this ship from leaving port at all costs. By the time *Bismarck* was sunk in May 1941, it was clear that Hitler did not want to risk his newest ship for no reason, so *Tirpitz* found herself sitting in Norwegian fjords and there she would be at anchor for the next few years.

Although she had come under air attack previously, her location at Kåfjord was somewhere that they figured was safe. Therefore, the Royal Navy had to come up with an innovative plan to attack the ship unexpectedly. This is where a new plan was devised – midget submarines.

Known as X-craft, these 51-foot-long mini-subs would be crewed by four people, but the mission and the training would be conducted in absolute secrecy. In a remote Scottish location, the crews were put through their paces and got to grips with the cramped conditions of the craft if they wanted to make this mission a success. Squashed together in this tiny tin can there was no way they would sail alone across the North Sea and up to the target. Therefore, they would be towed by regular submarines until the time was right to launch the attack.

Originally it was planned to attack three warships at once – *Tirpitz*, *Scharnhorst* and *Lützow* – but this was changed to just *Tirpitz* when it was found that *Scharnhorst* had sailed and the submarine sent to attack *Lützow* was lost on the way, as was one of the others. Of the six that had set out to attack the three ships, *X5*, *X6* and *X7* were cleared for attack on 20 September 1943 and the crews were swapped over ready for them to make their final journey across to the fjord. In charge of these craft were Lieutenant Henty Henty-Creer of *X5*, Lieutenant Donald Cameron of *X6* and Lieutenant Basil Place of *X7*. Each commander would have two officers and an artificer each.

The three subs slowly made their way unseen through Nazi-controlled Norwegian waters, careful not to be seen and giving the game away. They knew that *Tirpitz* was heavily defended by weapons and anti-submarine netting and there could even be mines along the way. Nighttime was when they would hide and recharge batteries before setting off again the following morning.

As the evening of 22 September came, the three craft moved into position, the anti-submarine netting being opened to let a ship through and so allowing the X-craft to sneak in close behind. It was now or never for the mission, each sub slowly manoeuvring underneath the hull of the huge battleship where they would drop their charges.

The explosives were in special containers shaped like the sides of the submarine, attached to both port and starboard side so it conformed to the shape of the hull. When they were released from inside the sub, they would simply fall away and land on the seabed below and the submarine would be free to make its escape.

But things like this never do go according to plan and although *X6* and *X7* dropped their charges, they were spotted by the ship and attacked. The subs were forced to surface and surrender; six of the eight crew were pulled out alive and taken on board the *Tirpitz*. As they were being questioned it was noticed that one of the men was constantly looking at his watch. It was then it was revealed that there were a number of timed explosive charges placed under the hull and that they would be detonating very soon.

The crew attempted to move the *Tirpitz* out of the way but it was too late. Two of the charges detonated and caused serious damage to the hull, letting water in and flooding compartments below. The damage caused by the X-Craft raid was enough to put *Tirpitz* out of action for several months.

Tirpitz would be moved once again to Tromsø where, in November 1944, she was once again attacked for the final time by heavy bombers in a raid that saw the ship take direct hits from Tallboy bombs where she took a considerable amount of damage and capsized at her anchorage. Over 900 German sailors lost their lives.

The submariners who took part in the X-craft raid in *X6* and *X7* were all honoured, the two captains receiving the Victoria Cross; three others received the Distinguished Service Order and one the Conspicuous Gallantry Medal. But for *X5* there was a Mention in Despatches for her commanding officer Lieutenant Henty-Creer. This is where a mystery surrounds what happened to this sub, last seen heading towards the operation.

At no point has any proof surfaced that they got near the battleship or laid any charges. Several expeditions have attempted to locate the wreck of *X5* but have failed to find any trace of the sub and her four crew. Minehunters HMS *Quorn* and HMS *Blyth* have done a sonar sweep of the area of the anchorage and found that a charge still on the seabed came from *X6*.

So where is *X5*? Did she even make it to the anchorage or was it spotted and damaged in an escape attempt? Mechanical failure is a possibility, considering they had already lost several craft on the way over from Britain to Norway, but if it had been enemy action before the attack commenced then it would have given prior warning to *Tirpitz* of a submarine attack. If it had been afterwards then there would be records of it.

It is highly likely that *X5* sank before the attack commenced. How or why will not be answered until the wreck is finally found. For many years campaigners have sought to have Henty-Creer awarded the Victoria Cross, but with no evidence that *X5* actually carried out the mission nobody can be sure what really went on.

For that question to be answered we have to wait until the wreck of *X5* is found in the icy cold waters or northern Norway.

Chapter 22

Orzel

After the First World War the submarine service became so much more sophisticated. By the time of the Second World War breaking out in 1939 these boats had come on in leaps and bounds compared to their predecessors twenty years previously. But from then on submarines had to have two things when on a mission – silence and secrecy. It is these two elements that meant that, in some cases, a submarine would head out on a mission and never be seen again. When a ship sinks it will leave debris floating on the surface, possibly fire and a life raft full of survivors. But when a submarine is lost everything is already underwater, so most of the parts do not float to the surface, unless it is oil or fuel, of course.

With the exact position never being known and the fact that a submarine has sunk not being realised until they fail to report in or show up at a rendezvous, many wartime subs have been just marked down as 'missing' until something could be confirmed. One such submarine is the Polish Navy's *Orzel* (Eagle in English).

Built in The Netherlands and launched in February 1939, this 275-foot-long submarine displaced 1,110 tons and could do 19 knots on the surface (9 knots submerged). On the upper deck forward was a 105mm deck gun as well as several smaller guns that were used for anti-aircraft defence, but her main armament were the twelve torpedo tubes, forward, aft and around the waist. With a crew of sixty, she was commissioned on 2 February 1939 and would operate mostly in the Baltic Sea.

When Nazi Germany invaded Poland on 1 September 1939 the Polish Navy fled to Britain where it could be saved from being taken over as well as fight on on the side of the Allies against the invaders of their homeland. *Orzel* had sailed and attempted to attack a German warship in the Baltic but was damaged along the way and so headed to Estonia for repairs. At the insistence of Germany, Estonian troops boarded the sub and confiscated her equipment and some of her torpedoes, but not before an act of sabotage prevented the crane from taking them all out.

On 18 September 1939, while their captain was in a local hospital being treated for a medical condition, the rest of the crew made a daring escape from the port. After overpowering the dockyard guards and coming under fire, *Orzel* ran aground in the harbour. After blowing her ballast tanks to make her lighter, the sub managed to manoeuvre into the Gulf of Finland, dropped off two dockyard workers whom they had brought along as hostages in Sweden and headed south towards their next destination – Great Britain.

With no charts or radio (they had all been taken by the Estonians) the sub managed to navigate all the way down to the bottom of the Baltic, around Denmark and into the North Sea, relying on landmarks and lighthouses along the way until finally they were free. But, with no wireless, they were attacked by forces from both sides as she couldn't identify herself as being a friendly force.

The whole incident with *Orzel* gave Russia an excuse for invading Estonia and blaming *Orzel* for sinking a tanker along the way (which it did not do). After forty days at sea the sub managed to make repairs to a radio and transmit a message off the coast of Scotland where a Royal Navy warship came out to escort her into harbour – much to the surprise of the British who thought she had been sunk weeks before.

Orzel was taken into the British fleet and used in the Norwegian campaign in 1940, sinking a German troop carrier named *Rio de Janeiro* on 8 April. She had ordered the ship to stop and surrender, but although the vessel stopped, it would not surrender, so *Orzel* fired torpedoes into the side of the *Rio de Janeiro* and the ship went down; around 200 people were killed.

The sub continued on her patrols and attempted more attacks on German warships, but without success, returning to port soon after.

Her seventh patrol in the North Sea began on 23 May 1940 when she set sail, her mission changing slightly at the start of June when she had orders to patrol the area around Denmark and Norway. But she was never heard from again. Her due date back to Rosyth came and went with no word from the *Orzel* and her crew.

No wreckage was ever found, nor was there any news of an attack on, or any trace of what happened to, this submarine. The only thing to go on is the theory that, not long after leaving port, she struck a mine and sank while submerged. Because of this then she could be anywhere from the east coast of Scotland to the Skagerrak.

Many theories as to where she sank have come to light. The British had a minefield that they had only just laid and many ships still hadn't been informed of its existence, but a German minefield was also on her route although it was not known about until charts were seized from a U-boat a year later.

So, with no real knowledge of where *Orzel* sank, it seems that looking for this wreck would be like searching for a needle in a haystack. But this is exactly what is being done.

Several expeditions have joined the hunt for the wreck of *Orzel*. Her story is now that of legend, especially the escape from Estonia and how the crew managed to get her all the way back to Britain as they did. Although at the time of writing, the wreck has not been found, searchers have found other wrecks along the way including HMS *Narwhal* which was sunk 150 miles from the Scottish coast during the Norwegian campaign in 1940. When the searchers came across a submarine, they believed the search for *Orzel* was over, but when it was identified as *Narwhal* it was bittersweet – *Orzel* was still lost but *Narwhal* is now found, along with three other previously unidentified shipwrecks.

With new expeditions being planned to search for the missing *Orzel*, it is safe to say that it is only a matter of time before the mystery of what happened to this heroic submarine is solved once and for all.

Chapter 23

U–47

There have been few submarine missions in the chronicles of underwater warfare that have propelled the boat and her crew into the history books, but the story of *U–47* is one that was an incredible act of cunning and bravery. Not only that, but, under Günther Prien, the submarine would become one of the most successful U-boats of the war.

Born in the German state of Prussia in 1908, Günther Prien had already gained his master's certificate at the age of 24, having, since boyhood, spent many years at sea, including experience on sailing ships. In 1933 he joined the German navy and went to sea on submarines. At the start of the war in 1939 he was already in command of *U–47*. The U-boat had been launched in Kiel in 1930 and was 753 tons, 218 feet long with a crew of up to 60 personnel.

Within days of war breaking out, Prien sank a ship in the Baltic, claiming the second vessel sunk in the Second World War. He went on to sink several more ships before returning to port. Already *U–47* was making a name for itself. The next patrol would cement that name firmly in the annals of history.

It was the night of 13 October 1939 and Scapa Flow was in darkness, the Home Fleet of the Royal Navy at anchor protected by a barrage of anti-submarine netting, blockships and natural hazards. But for *U–47* it was a time to prove that Hitler's U-boats could go anywhere. Although not all the fleet was in the area at the time, the battleship *Royal Oak* was a very large target and so Prien lined up his submarine for an attack.

As midnight crossed over into 14 October, Prien carefully positioned his vessel near the *Royal Oak*. While the rest of the ships in Scapa Flow were sleeping soundly, *U–47* fired her torpedoes. Only one, severing an anchor chain. It was believed to have been either an internal explosion or an air attack. The second salvo was loosed off twenty minutes later, Prien having re-positioned his boat. Three torpedoes slammed into the side of the battleship.

As sailors fought to survive, Prien made his escape. Just thirteen minutes after the first torpedo strike, *Royal Oak* was upside down on the seabed, 835 of her crew were killed, or died later from their injuries. By the time the British had realised that a submarine had somehow got into the base, Prien and his crew were already racing away to safety. On 17 October Prien arrived back in Germany to a hero's welcome where he was awarded the Knight's Cross of the Iron Cross, the first submariner to receive that decoration and only the second member of the Kriegsmarine.

But *U-47* was not done yet, for she went out on her next patrol a month later and sank even more ships in the convoys. By this time, Prien was one of the top three U-boat aces (the others were Joachim Schepke and Otto Kretschmer). Prien's reputation had skyrocketed. He eventually took his boat out on nine patrols and sank thirty ships in just less than eighteen months and that is not including *Royal Oak*. Other ships were damaged but managed to make it to safety. Among the ships sunk by *U-47* was the liner *Arandora Star*, but what nobody was to know is that it was carrying German and Italian internees who were being shipped from Britain to Canada. Over 800 people on board were killed.

Sailing on 20 February 1941, this was Prien's tenth patrol in *U-47* and there was no reason to believe it would not be another success, including some prisoners of war. Departing from Lorient, he intercepted a convoy and sank two ships just days later, other German units moving into position later to cause even more devastation.

On 7 March Prien attacked a convoy but his luck had finally run out when one of the escort ships dashed to his position. Overnight into 8 March the submarine was being chased and bombarded with depth charges. Reports say that the submarine rose to the surface and exploded, others say that there is no record of what happened. Either way, *U-47* and her entire crew of forty-five were lost forever.

The death of Prien was kept secret until 23 May when Churchill announced it in the House of Commons. Germany was forced to admit not long after that they had lost one of their best U-boat aces.

Where the submarine vanished is one of those questions that has never been answered and were the reports of the sinking of a submarine that day true? The name of the submarine and her captain have gone down in history for sure, but with such a famous submarine it is strange how no one has offered to hunt for the wreck.

Prien's life has been the subject of several books, a war movie and TV specials. His name is listed along with his forty-four crew members at the U-boat memorial in Kiel and there is a street named after him in the municipality of Schonberg, in northern Germany.

Today the battleship *Royal Oak* still sits at the bottom of Scapa Flow; the passage that Prien used that night is permanently sealed up with a bridge blocking the entryway and known as Churchill Barrier.

The loss of Günther Prien and *U-47* was a huge blow to German morale and the navy in general. Before long, they had suffered the loss of two more of their best when one was sunk and another captured. By May 1943 technology, better tactics and weaponry had helped turn the tide in the Battle of the Atlantic and the race to victory in the Second World War had finally to favour the Allies.

Chapter 24

U-110

The Second World War was a time not only for unrestricted warfare but weapons innovation and, as the conflict progressed and spread around the globe, it became apparent that the mechanics used to fight it were becoming more and more sophisticated. Radar and sonar technology had developed, as had the guns and explosive charges used to sink the German U-boats once they had been located. In many cases, the future outcome of the war was a competition to see not who could win the armed battles but who could win with their minds.

One major piece of equipment used by the Germans was, above all others, a high priority target for the Allies. This was a small encryption machine resembling a complicated looking typewriter with a number of dials and switches that could encode a normal message and transmit it to forces on the front line where a similar contraption would decode it into plain language. Its name was Enigma and it was the biggest headache that the Allies needed to crack.

Variations of the machine were given to all forces and civilian services. The exact position of the dials, cables and connectors would determine on the settings for the day and it was said to be virtually unbreakable. At a mansion known as Bletchley Park near Milton Keynes a team of codebreakers were working day and night to try to crack the code. Their task was enormous – the settings of Enigma meant that there were a possible 159 million million million different combinations that would take hundreds of years to figure out, even with a team of highly-trained mathematicians. The worst part was that the codes changed at midnight, so they would have to start all over again.

But things were about to change and a little bit of luck and a lot of hard work and sacrifice were about to play out off the coast of Iceland. The submarine *U-110* had departed from its naval base at the French port of Lorient on 15 April 1941, had already sunk one ship and was chasing convoys across the Atlantic. Launched on 25 August 1940, the sub was 251 feet long and displaced just over 1,000 tons on the surface, a crew of forty-seven making up the ship's company on this particular patrol. The sub had already had a success on previous missions when they damaged a ship although they would have preferred to sink it.

The commanding officer was *Kapitänleutnant* Fritz-Julius Lemp who, at the age of 28 had already made a name for himself in the German navy. Just eight hours after the declaration of war with Germany he had fired torpedoes from his submarine *U-30* at the liner *Athenia*, sinking her and causing outrage across both sides of the Atlantic. Now he was back on patrol and taking *U-110* to cause more chaos with the convoys.

On 9 May 1941 Lemp saw a convoy in his sights and lined up for attack. The two ships *Esmond* and *Bengore Head* were hit and sank, but Lemp seemed to have left his periscope up for too long, most likely to confirm that he had sunk the ships. The U-boat was spotted and the escort ships altered course to attack *U-110*.

Two warships were gaining on her. The corvette HMS *Aubrietia* scanned the area using asdic equipment and once they believed they had found her *Aubrietia* and the destroyer HMS *Broadway* went in for the kill with depth charges. Joined by HMS *Bulldog* the submarine was eventually caught up in the multitude of underwater explosions and Lemp was forced to order the submarine to surface.

Bulldog manoeuvred into position to ram the submarine and Lemp ordered the crew to abandon. At the last moment *Bulldog* turned away and, realising that the submarine was still on the surface and that it was now in a position to be captured rather than sunk, Lemp swam towards the submarine as quickly as possible to ensure the secret documents could be destroyed. Lemp was last seen trying to save one of his crew; he had already saved three.

In the meantime, survivors of the sub were picked up by the Royal Navy ships, thirty-two in all out of the forty-seven who had been on board. Some of the survivors stated later that the British ships opened fire on them in the water and killed many of those who did not make it.

A boarding party was organised on the *Bulldog* and a boat was sent over to the damaged *U-110* to see if there was anything that could be used as intelligence. When they arrived on board, they found a machine that turned out to be an Enigma machine, complete with up-to-date settings books.

With the U-boat now wallowing in the seas it was decided to hook up a tow and attempt to bring it back to shore but, as time went on, *U-110* flooded further due to the damage it had already received and eventually sank in the middle of the ocean off Iceland.

The capture of the German crew was not made public. They were interned as prisoners of war in Canada but nothing was said of where they had come from. For everyone watching the state of the war the *U-110* was simply 'sunk at sea' in an operation like hundreds of other German submarines during the war. In the meantime, Enigma and its code books were rushed back to Britain and sent to Bletchley Park where grateful codebreakers could use them to break the messages sent by Enigma. Although this was one of many ciphers that had to be broken, it was an important one, nonetheless, and it is said that the work being done at this unit helped shorten the war by around two years.

Eventually, in 1974, the secret of the capture of the Enigma from *U-110* was made public and over the years the world has learned of the incredible work carried out by the codebreakers, the name of Alan Turing being in the forefront of the fight behind closed doors. Enigma itself has been a star of a number of fictional movies such as *Enigma* (a Robert Harris novel of the same name) and *U-571* (which caused controversy over Hollywood being accused of re-writing history). But there has never been a film released about the capture of *U-110* or the cover up following the realisation that this was an incredible discovery.

Although the incident has featured in several books and is today well known, there are no plans in place to search for the wreck of this historically significant vessel. Today the names of those who died on board the sub are inscribed on the U-boat Memorial in the German port of Kiel, along with the tens of thousands of other submariners who never returned home after their mission.

Chapter 25

Surcouf

There are few incidents at sea whereby a modern day vessel is lost with no word on where exactly it has gone. These days a shipwreck hunt would take place until the missing vessel was located, although during the wartime period there were so many being lost to enemy action that it would be too much to be able to account for every submarine at any one time. For those that are never confirmed as being sunk it is simply a case of it being a mystery and leaving it at that. In the decade before this book was written, there were two submarine losses, the Argentine *San Juan* and the Indonesian *Nanggala*, both of which sank with all hands in 2017 and 2021 respectively.

In those cases, a search for the subs and the investigation could determine why the vessel was lost and at least give answers to the relatives of those serving on board. But during periods of conflict, and with limited technology, the attention given to submarines going missing under non-warfare circumstances was very limited.

The French submarine *Surcouf* is one of these vessels. A huge submarine, she was launched in Cherbourg in 1929 and commissioned into the French navy in 1934. A very unusual looking craft, she sported the usual conning tower, but then in front of that was a single turret mounting two 8-inch guns, making her look like a cross between a sub and a cruiser. She was designed to be both a surface raider and a reconnaissance vessel as well as carrying out the usual duties an attack submarine must manage. At 361 feet long, she was armed with machine guns for anti-aircraft fire and ten torpedo tubes, at the same time carrying a floatplane stored in a hangar on the aft deck. There had never been a submarine like it before. Although *Surcouf* was meant to be the first of several in a class of submarines, no others were built.

When war broke out and France was taken over by Nazi Germany, the *Surcouf* escaped to Britain and found refuge in Plymouth. The French fleet was destroyed at Mers el Kebir, Oran, by the Royal Navy in 1940 rather than let it fall into enemy hands. In the meantime, all French warships

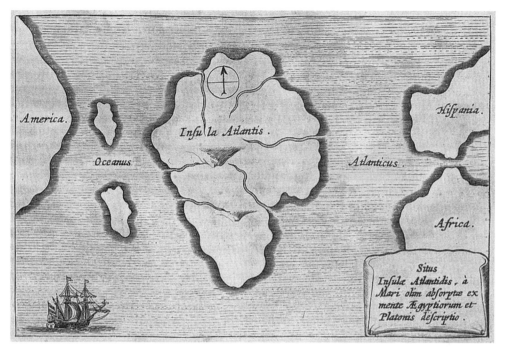

Map of Atlantis by Athanasius Kircher, 1678.

Captain Briggs of the *Mary Celeste*.

Mary Celeste under her former name *Amazon* in 1861.

Flannan Isles Lighthouse photographed in 2012. (*Chris Downer*)

The *Bonhomme Richard* fights HMS *Serapis* in the Battle of Flamborough Head, 1779.

The loss of the USS *Cyclops* became the greatest mystery of the United States Navy. (*US Navy Yard*)

The battle-cruiser HMS *Courageous*. (*Surgeon Oscar Parkes*)

HMS *Courageous* after her conversion to an aircraft carrier. (*Royal Navy*)

HMS *Glorious* as a battle-cruiser.

HMS *Glorious* as an aircraft carrier.

The battleship HMS *Barham* was a veteran of the Battle of Jutland. (*U.S. Naval Historical Center*)

HMS *Barham*'s magazine explodes after being torpedoed in the Mediterranean in 1941.

Commanded by Lord Mountbatten, HMS *Kelly* was lost off Crete in 1941.

The battleship USS *Oklahoma* in 1917.

USS *Oklahoma* capsized in Pearl Harbor following the attack by Japanese aircraft, 7th December 1941. (*US Navy*)

USS *Oklahoma* in 1947 following the salvage operation and ready for scrapping. (*US Navy*)

The LCU *Foxtrot 4* from HMS *Fearless*, sunk in an air raid during the Falklands campaign, 1982.

HMS *Fearless* had four LCU landing craft that would be carried in her stern and four smaller LCVPs carried externally. *Fearless* is seen here in this 1996 photo. (*US Navy*)

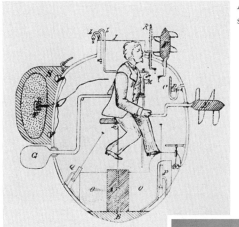

An 1885 sketch of David Bushnell's submarine *Turtle*.

X-24 in a museum, similar to the ones that carried out the attack on the German battleship *Tirpitz*. (*Geni*)

St Romanus

Kingston Peridot

Ross Cleveland

The three Hull fishing vessels lost in the Triple Trawler Tragedy of 1968 – *St Romanus, Kingston Peridot* and the *Ross Cleveland*.

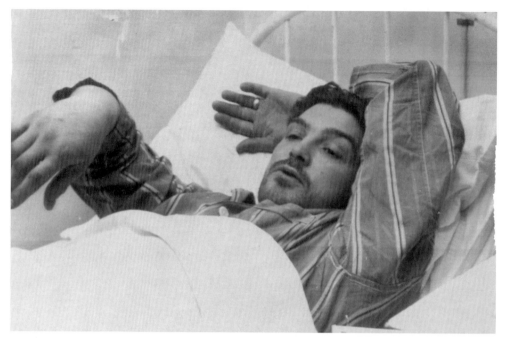

Harry Eddom in an Icelandic hospital after being the sole survivor from the sinking *Ross Cleveland*.

SS *Waratah*. (*Gaverial Nissim Bar*)

The *Waratah* vanished with no survivors in 1909; this contemporary postcard shows her in rough seas.

Emlyn Brown has made several searches for the wreck of the *Waratah* and at one point believed he had found the lost ship, but this turned out to be the SS *Nailsea Meadow*. (*Emlyn Brown*)

The Leyland Line ship *Californian* on the morning of *Titanic*'s sinking. (*Author unknown but taken from Carpathia*).

A memorial to the lives lost on board the *Hans Hedtoft* after she struck an iceberg and sank on her maiden voyage in 1959.

The *Lakonia* is seen here in 1948 under her previous name, the Dutch liner *Johan van Oldenbarnevelt*. (*Marine Luchtvaart Dienst Indië*)

The airship *Italia* was the pride of Italy and her designer Umberto Nobile. (*Bundesarchiv*)

Despite Roald Amundsen and Umberto Nobile not getting along, the Norwegian Arctic explorer vanished during a search for the missing airship and has never been seen since.

A memorial to the victims of the airship *Italia* in Tromso, Norway. (*Sparrow*)

The disappearance of Amelia Earhart is still one of the biggest unsolved mysteries of aviation.

Hull-born Amy Johnson broke many flying records until she was lost in a crash in the Thames Estuary in 1941 during war service. (*National Library of Australia*)

The US Navy blimp *L-8* went out on a routine patrol and returned with nobody on board, crashing into a San Francisco housing estate. (*National Naval Aviation Museum, Florida*)

The gondola from *L-8* survives today and is displayed at the National Naval Aviation Museum, Florida. (*Photo courtesy of National Aviation Museum*)

A US Army photo of band leader Glenn Miller who vanished over the English Channel on the way to a concert in 1944.

The US Navy assists in the search for Malaysia Airlines flight MH370. (*US Navy*)

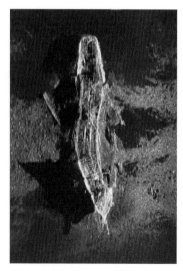

A shipwreck discovered in December 2015 during the search for MH370. (*ATSB*)

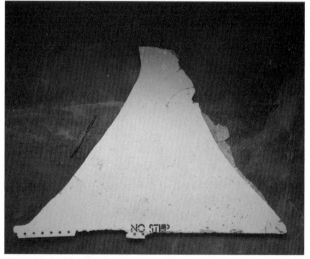

MH370 wreckage washed ashore on the beaches of Mozambique over a year after the airliner went missing. (*ATSB*)

in Britain were boarded by armed teams to make sure that any potential enemy combatants did not have ideas about fighting for the Vichy French and helping the Germans. But the French navy were not happy with being boarded and taken over by the British despite them offering safe harbour. This led to a skirmish on *Surcouf* which left four dead (three British and one French) before the sub was eventually seized. The plan was to make sure the crew were all fighting for the same side (the Allies) and that there was no danger of *Surcouf* being used to supply the enemy or used against their own convoys.

Eventually, she was refitted by the British and handed over to the Free French Navy although both sides accused each other of working for the enemy, Vichy France, but with UK liaison personnel on board and a crew of over 100 men she was eventually sent across the Atlantic to Canada to conduct convoy escort and protection duties. The submarine was later Involved in the liberation of the islands of St Pierre and Miquelon, just off Newfoundland in 1941.

On 12 February 1942 *Surcouf* departed Bermuda bound for the Panama Canal ready to head into the Pacific. On board were 130 crew, including four Royal Navy personnel, and there were rumours of her heading to the island of Martinique to assist in taking back the island for the Free French, but this was just a rumour.

But *Surcouf* was never seen again. On 12 February 1942 her last communications were received and then that was it. The fact that submarines tend to operate in radio silence meant that, once they had submerged, they could be travelling for several days before meeting with their doom ... or they could submerge and encounter a problem straightaway. The distance between last reported position and location of the wreck could be hundreds or even thousands of miles away.

One clue as to the fate of the *Surcouf* is the American freighter *Thompson Lykes*, which reported striking a submerged object off Panama on 18 February but could not say anything other than that. An alternative explanation was in the records of the 6th Heavy Bomber Group based in Panama which record an attack they made on a large submarine on 19 February in roughly the same area. As there was no German activity reported in this area, this is one of two theories as to the loss of the *Surcouf* that do hold up. Other theories involving them helping the Nazis and being found out are unfounded.

The announcement of the loss of *Surcouf* was not made for another three months and it was January 1945 that the collision with the freighter was reported freely, although there are several aspects that both match with the collision theory and rule it out at the same time. Another theory is that the collision only damaged the sub and it was forced to surface where the bombers caught her the day after and finished the job.

There have been many theories as to what went on but, whatever the truth, the sinking of the *Surcouf* remains the world's worst submarine disaster, the loss of the nuclear USS *Thresher* coming a very close second with 129 killed. The story of the loss of the *Surcouf* is overshadowed by the modern nuclear submarines and an online search for 'world's worst submarine disaster' will give you the *Thresher* and *Kursk* as they are more memorable, but *Surcouf* still holds that tragic record.

In the French port of Cherbourg where *Surcouf* was built is a monument at the end of a pier. Shaped like a conning tower with periscope, a green plaque, with all 130 names inscribed, pays tribute to those who lost their lives on the submarine on eternal patrol for a Free France and a liberated Europe.

Part IV
Merchant Ships

Chapter 26

Royal Merchant

Priceless artefacts, gold and treasure are always reasons for people searching for lost ships. There have been so many treasure ships come to grief over the last few hundred years, but very few of them are found. In the 1980s Mel Fisher made worldwide headlines with his discovery of the Spanish ship *Nuestra Senora de Atocha* which had been wrecked off the coast of Florida. The incredible artefacts, jewels and gold that were brought up from the seabed made him a legend overnight. But few realise that there are still many of those treasure ships still out there waiting to be found.

One of these missing ships is the *Royal Merchant*, built in Deptford in 1627 and fairly small in comparison to today's general cargo ships at just 157 feet long. Carrying thirty-two cannon and a crew of fewer than sixty, she made regular voyages around the Caribbean trading with Spanish colonies and spent two years in that area before making her way towards Spain itself, a country that was then at peace with England.

Only fourteen years after her launch, *Royal Merchant* was in bad condition. She was leaking heavily and the pumps were constantly trying to get the water out of the holds. Pulling into Cadiz she was given another job along the way after a nearby Spanish ship caught fire and couldn't take her cargo to Antwerp. The captain of the *Royal Merchant*, John Limbrey, offered to head in that direction for a price and so all the treasure that was destined for Belgium was loaded onto his ship. Repairs were carried out on the leaks that had caused so much trouble heading across the Atlantic and they were ready for the last leg of their journey home.

Together with her sister ship *Dover Merchant*, the *Royal Merchant* continued to have problems with the ship leaking and as she passed the southern coast of England the pumps stopped working altogether.

On 23 September 1641 the ship could take no more as the seas got rough, more water flooded into the holds and the crew knew it was time to abandon ship. *Dover Merchant* was close by and was able to pick up survivors but out of the fifty-eight people on board only forty of them were saved, including the captain.

The loss of such a large amount of treasure was felt in the city of Antwerp when they realised that they could not pay their soldiers. The ship had sunk with one of the richest treasure hordes of all time on board.

This immense amount of lost treasure is estimated to be somewhere in the region of £1 billion, but this is only based on what is thought to be on board. Precious stones like gems, pearls and jewels, together with gold bullion and thousands of coins, mean that when this wreck is found the discoverer will be very rich – if it can be recovered.

In 2007 there was a rumour that the wreck had been located when an announcement was made by Odyssey Marine Exploration that a shipwreck had been found in the eastern area of the Atlantic with over half a million silver coins and various other riches which had littered the seabed around it.

The operation was conducted in secret in the hope that the discovery would not be hijacked by other companies. In the meantime, footage released of the treasure being flown to the United States showed boxes full of coins, proving that this was an immense discovery. But that was where the problems started for Odyssey.

While the press were suggesting that this was the discovery of the *Royal Merchant*, Odyssey had codenamed the wreck 'Black Swan', but the Spanish government found that what they had in fact located was the warship *Nuestra Senora de las Mercedes*, sunk in 1804 after a battle with the British in the exact location where the search vessel had been conducting operations just before the announcement. Legal wrangling ensued for several years until finally it was confirmed that it was in fact the *Mercedes* wreck and, in 2013, the 14.5 tons of treasure was handed over to the Spanish after a court order telling them to do so. Looking at the location of the wreck on a chart it is clear that this was nowhere near the location that *Royal Merchant* had gone down. However, it did bring the lost ship back into the forefront of missing ships and her story was once again told.

While losing the battle over the Black Swan Project, Odyssey did, however, acquire rights to a TV series called *Treasure Quest* that followed them on some of their other wreck searches. While many of them were already found or already documented, they did dedicate one episode to the wreck of the *Royal Merchant*.

While the mystery wreck was identified off Spain, the wreck of the *Royal Merchant* still remains on the seabed today, approximately thirty-five miles from the Cornish coast. Perhaps it is only a matter of time now before we see another scene such as we did when Mel Fisher found his *Atocha*, the priceless riches from 400 years ago dominating a museum. But we have to take many stories with a pinch of salt as much as we all want to believe that it would be loaded to the brim with treasure.

Did *Royal Merchant* have as much as what was rumoured? Such a small ship, yet packed with so much heavy gold from not only Spain but from its own trading voyages over the last two years of its career? One has to wonder why such a leaky ship was given the task of taking all of this precious cargo across the Bay of Biscay, notorious for rough seas, when so much was at stake if it was lost. There are two possible scenarios, the first being that it was insured for loss and that the owners were given a hefty pay out when in actual fact it was in a bad state of repair and perhaps not concealing any treasure at all. But let's not forget eighteen people died on board that ship so, if this was the case, it was a high price to pay risking life and limb.

Or it may have literally been the fact that they had made repairs and honestly believed that the ship was fine and that the repairs would be good enough to get back to Britain via Antwerp. Whatever the truth it would be interesting to see if this ship is as treasure-laden as the legends say, or whether it is just another shipwreck with a good story to tell.

Chapter 27

General Grant

Another treasure ship that has long remained lost is that of the *General Grant*, although its location should be known, considering its fate against the rocks of New Zealand's Auckland Islands. Built in Maine, USA, in 1864, this three-masted barque of just over 1,000 tons was only two years old when she met with disaster. She was 179.5 feet long and on 4 May 1866 had sailed out of Hobson's Bay with a cargo of wool and skins as well as gold and various other precious items. Carrying fifty-eight passengers and a crew of twenty-five, some of the passengers being local gold miners, the *General Grant* was making her way from Melbourne, Australia to London, a journey of many weeks of stormy seas and long days ahead.

But the ship didn't get as far as New Zealand when, just nine days into the journey, they came upon the Auckland Islands just off the west coast. Unfortunately, the lack of wind meant that the ship could not steer out of the way of the rocks in time and, very late into the night of 13 May, the ship grounded onto the shore and into a huge cave. An unusual situation to be in; the ship could not get out of the cave and the rising tide meant that the masts were now touching the top of the cave roof and slowly causing them to be forced downwards through the hull.

The natural swell of the sea had a mast smack the roof and act like a giant hammer constantly banging the mast down as if it was driving a huge nail into the ship from above. Chunks of the ship were flying round as those on board were too afraid to launch the lifeboats in the dark. As daylight broke three boats were made ready and one left the cave to try to find a landing point where the survivors would be able to head to.

While all this was going on, the ship itself was sinking in the cave, water flooding the holds below and, in the end, the third boat full of passengers simply floated off the aft end of the ship. The swell was increasing noticeably and the three boats could only watch in horror as it was found that there was nowhere nearby to head for: it was rocks in every direction. The boat still in the cave was now getting swamped in the swell and sank, only three people from that boat able to swim to safety to one of the other boats.

By now fifteen people were dead, including the captain and six passengers, the survivors in two boats now in a fight for survival. What happened next was an incredible tale of survival against all odds as the two boats rowed to a nearby island, aptly named Disappointment Island, an uninhabited piece of land with natural habitats of various wildlife, but not a place for survivors to land in the hope of being rescued.

Three days later they rowed to the main island of Auckland and aimed for the natural harbour of Port Ross where they became castaways stuck on an island with no other humans. Watching the horizon for a rescue ship that never came, their only view being a hut nearby, the group split up into teams to try to aid survival and explore as much of the area as possible. But, as the months went on, the survivors started to succumb to illness and one group of four put to sea in a boat with no navigation equipment or charts and were never seen again. Those still on the island made fires to keep warm but had very little shelter from the cold winds and torrential rain and wore only the clothes in which they had survived the shipwreck.

In the end, there were just ten survivors left. By then they had moved to Enderby Island where, eventually, a passing ship, the whaling ship *Amherst*, noticed them and rescued the bedraggled castaways. They had lived off wild animals such as seals and pigs, managed to grow potatoes and herd goats, but the date was 21 November 1867, eighteen months after the *General Grant* had been lost.

Due to the loss of the *General Grant* and several other wrecks in that area of islands, the government of New Zealand erected a series of huts on the uninhabited islands for future castaways and arranged regular visits by rescue teams in case of an unknown shipwreck so at least any future victims would have a fighting chance of survival. To have eighty-three people on board *General Grant* taken down to just ten was unacceptable when the wreck itself only killed fifteen of that number.

The wreck of the *General Grant* itself and its vast quantity of treasure was never found, although the rough area of the shipwreck is known about. From the moment the wreck was known about there have been searches for the remains, but each one has failed in its attempt to unlock the secret of the lost vessel.

Although the survivors' stories have been quite clear and the locations very specific, the location of the wreck has eluded treasure hunters ever since. Even as recently as 2022 an expedition was sent out to find the gold. Bill Day is a treasure seeker who has already made over two dozen attempts to locate the wreck and yet he, too, has been left without a clue as to where the remains of *General Grant* lie.

Day came to the conclusion that a cliff may have collapsed in the last 150 years and buried the cave and the wreck forever. But it is not the lure of treasure that interests him. In fact he has shown a passion for mapping the wreck site and leaving the site initially untouched, instead concentrating on an archaeological excavation where the artefacts would be preserved after photographs were taken and the entire site treated with respect.

Excitement took hold on a previous expedition when his team found a shipwreck in a cave. Incredibly, that was not the *General Grant* but a different wreck from even earlier still which he later identified.

So, the wreck of the *General Grant* is still missing, lost at sea with a hoard of treasure, a New Zealand version of the *Atocha*, the remains of a proud ship and a precious cargo scattered among the rocks. If Day's theory is true and a cliff collapse has buried the wreck, this becomes reminiscent of the final scene in the film *The Goonies* when (spoiler alert) the pirate ship *Inferno* is found in perfect condition full of treasure.

But while Hollywood provides the entertainment, history tells us that shipwrecks in a cave are few and far between and the chances of them being in top condition is impossible, but this is not to say that the cave in which the *General Grant* came to grief hasn't helped preserve the site for future generations.

It is just possible that the future may show that, due to the navigation charts being terrible back in 1866, that the *General Grant* may still be found.

Chapter 28

Carroll A. Deering

T his next ship is a classic shipwreck story and one that is not lost but comes with a bizarre twist that has baffled investigators for over a century and still continues to spark interest today. This is the story of the five-masted schooner *Carroll A. Deering*, a cargo vessel that was launched in 1919 from Maine, USA and owned by the G.G. Deering Co. who had the vessel named after the owner's son.

She was an impressive sight, at 255 feet long and 1,879 tons. She carried only eleven crew but could be filled with precious cargo, the luxuries on board designed to provide the crew with home comforts on what could be long journeys up and down the Atlantic coast of the American continent.

On 26 August 1920, on a voyage from Newport News, Virginia, the ship had not been at sea long when the captain, a war hero named William H. Merritt, fell seriously ill and the ship put into a Delaware port where he had to be taken off along with his son. They were replaced by two new crewmen, a Captain Willis B. Wormell, who was actually a 66-year-old retired mariner, along with a new first mate to replace the son.

The voyage was resumed on 8 September without incident and the ship arrived in Rio where the cargo was delivered. The ship didn't leave Rio until 2 December and arrived in Barbados for stores and supplies; it was here that the first sight of drama reared its head when the First Mate, Charles McLellan, had too much to drink and confided in a friend that he was finding the captain difficult to deal with. He was having to carry out navigational work, due to the captain's failing eyesight, but when he tried to discipline the crew the captain thought that he was undermining him by interfering with the skipper's duties. Threatening to 'get him' he was soon arrested, but on 9 January the captain bailed him out of jail and put the complaints behind him in order for the *Carroll A. Deering* to set sail for Hampton Roads.

The ship sailed, but a few weeks later it was sighted by the Cape Lookout Lightship off the North Carolina coast on 28 January 1921. The schooner hailed the vessel and told them that they had lost their anchors in a storm off Cape Fear and requested that the owners be notified of the loss. The problem was that their radio was not working and so this report could not be passed on. When Captain Jacobson, the lightship's keeper, looked over at the person hailing them he described him as having reddish hair, a foreign accent and being tall and thin. On the quarterdeck, there were people described as just 'milling around', which was never allowed. This was unorthodox but not that strange.

However, the following day the ship was sighted heading on a course towards a group of sandbars, known as the Diamond Shoals, off Cape Hatteras. Most likely they would turn as they came into view of the lighthouse nearby, although it was noted that not a single person was seen on the upper deck.

On 31 January the *Carroll A. Deering* was sighted by the Cape Hatteras Coastguard Station at dawn with all her sails set but fully aground on the Diamond Shoals. The weather was bad but still a rescue attempt was sent out. The seas were too rough and the rescuers beaten back and it would be another four days before a team could get over and board the vessel. But by the time the ship was boarded there was nobody on board.

Looking around the ship there was clear damage to the steering equipment and some of the navigation facilities, such as the binnacle. The ships two lifeboats were not there nor were the crew's personal possessions, the ship's log and various other navigation pieces. Food was being prepared in the galley, so whatever had happened it seemed that they had not had time to eat first.

A salvage mission was attempted but the ship was jammed on the reef and wasn't moving anytime soon. The only thing they could do was attach explosives to it and blow it up to prevent it becoming a navigation hazard. Chunks of the ship drifted ashore later on.

What had happened to the crew of the *Carroll A. Deering*? It was clear that they had voluntarily left the ship as the lifeboat was gone, although did all eleven crew leave in the boats? The investigation was launched by the US Government and very little information was forthcoming. What they did do though was check through the logs of other ships that had been in the area who all confirmed the state of the weather as being at hurricane strength. Coastguards confirmed this data also but this still did not explain why eleven people would leave a perfectly good ship in a storm onboard two lifeboats when the ship could simply sail to safety. She didn't have her anchor, but that didn't stop her changing course and sailing elsewhere or even completing the voyage as planned.

Another ship had disappeared in the same area at around the same time and an inquiry by investigators from Italy confirmed that the *Monte San Michele* had been in the same hurricane which was the likely cause for that loss.

A hoax message in a bottle three months later led to speculation that the ship had been hijacked by another ship's crew, but the finder of the bottle later admitted that he had written it himself hoping for attention that would lead to him getting a job at a nearby light station.

Another possible theory is that a nearby ship had rescued the crew, for the distress signals had been found to have been lit. Some suggested that they were taken off by the steamship *Hewitt*, but that ship, too, went down in the same storm with all hands. Could this have been a successful rescue but then the rescuers became victims themselves? It's possible.

In the end it was thought strongly that the vessel had been the victim of a mutiny, although with very little evidence to go on the theory that the crew simply abandoned ship when the vessel went aground and were swept out to sea was just as plausible. To this day there is no concrete explanation as to where the crew of the *Carroll A. Deering* went or what led to the ship being grounded on the Diamond Shoals: yet another mystery of the sea that may never be solved.

The wreckage of the broken ship was sticking out of the sandy shoal for many years and a photograph taken in the 1950s shows the capstan precariously balancing on top of broken deck supports. That capstan, as well as the ship's bell, were taken from the wreck and have since been placed on display at a museum in Cape Hatteras.

Of all the ships that have had mysterious happenings throughout history, the loss of this 'Ghost Ship of the Atlantic' has become one of the more popular subjects of discussion.

Chapter 29

Baychimo

As you have seen with quite a few stories in this book, the sea is full of surprises when it comes to drifting, crewless ships, vanishing ships and empty lighthouses. Another strange sighting out at sea was the cargo ship *Baychimo*. At the time of her loss, it didn't seem that her being abandoned would be cause for the attention she later received, attention that has lasted many years.

Launched in Sweden as the *Ångermanelfven* in 1914, she was 230 feet long and fitted out to resemble the rigging of a schooner. Owned by a German company, she was handed over to the British after the First World War as part of the reparations laid down in the Treaty of Versailles. Renamed *Baychimo*, she was taken over by the Hudson Bay Company and carried out her first trip under her new owners in 1921.

Baychimo found herself making a lot of trips in the Arctic regions until 1922 when she made a round-the-world trip, via the Panama Canal, from Scotland to Canada. Each journey she carried cargo to the western Arctic area and even carried passengers, although these were officially listed as crew due to the ship not being licensed to carry passengers.

In September 1931, as she was making her way back to Vancouver, she was caught in a blizzard off the northern coast of Alaska and the crew brought the ship to anchor to ride out the bad weather. By the time the storm had passed the ship was caught up in the ice that had formed around it and the crew had no choice but to build a camp next to it where they were able to burn wood when it was too much to try to heat the entire ship.

Each day that went by the crew would perform maintenance on the ship, chipping away at the ice to prevent damage and, in some cases, the crew were flown to Alaska and on to Vancouver. The weeks dragged on with no sign of the ship being able to float free, the very real danger of her being crushed evident at every stormy period.

By late November 1931, the ship had been stranded for two months and another storm was tearing through the camp. When it eventually cleared and the visibility had gone back to normal, the *Baychimo* was no longer there. With the assumption that the ship had been crushed by the ice and gone down, the crew started to make plans to leave the area, but soon word from an Inuit hunter told them that around forty-five miles away a ship was stuck in the ice and that was soon established to be *Baychimo*. She had broken free of the ice with nobody on board and had become stranded yet again in one piece.

Making the long trek across the freezing wasteland, the captain and crew soon found the ship stranded as before and boarded the vessel. Establishing that the *Baychimo* was no longer seaworthy, they took off as much as possible that they would need for survival to make their journey home and left her. The ship had taken so much damage from the ice and on her journey there, being hit by various chunks of ice along the way, that it was not worth saving and would soon sink.

It was March 1932 by the time the crew were flown back to Vancouver to sort out the paperwork that account for the loss of the ship and the cargo. That seemed to be the end of the story for them, but it was not long before there were reports of the ship being spotted in various locations near the Alaskan shores, this time adrift and floating on its own accord.

This is where the ship was turned into a legend as the 'Ghost Ship of the Arctic'. It would continue to be spotted, adrift and alone.

A year after she was abandoned, a group of people found her and boarded the vessel but an unexpected storm led to them being trapped on board for ten days until the storm cleared. Another boarding that same year saw that the ship was being stripped internally of many useful items that the local Inuits could use themselves. Further sightings of the ship a year later, and a salvage attempt in 1939, led to her being left to the ice floes once again. Already she had been adrift and abandoned for eight years.

During the Second World War she was sighted on several occasions but crews were unable to board her. As time passed, sightings of the *Baychimo* became fewer and fewer. A group of Inuit found her drifting alone in March 1962 along the Beaufort Sea and the last recorded sighting was that of her frozen in an ice pack in 1969, almost four decades after the crew had originally abandoned her.

Where she went from there is anybody's guess. Most likely the damage sustained to the ship eventually became too much and she sank somewhere in the Beaufort Sea. To drift for that length of time with no maintenance and a continuous battering by ice on the hull as well as being frozen in and crushed on so many occasions, it was inevitable that she would vanish at some point.

In 2006 the Alaskan government started to work on a new project to locate the thousands of ships that have been lost along the coast and *Baychimo* was one of them. While it is highly unlikely that she is still trapped in ice (but not impossible) the likelihood of her being found on the seabed may one day come to pass.

What was interesting in this incident was the number of photographs taken of the ship by her original crew when they were trapped in the ice, the black and white images of a bunch of people on a camp surrounded by ice and snow, the ship trapped and the crew working around it was reminiscent of the 1915 images of the *Endurance* which suffered the same fate in the Antarctic and which sank after being trapped.

Never before or since has there been a ghost ship quite like the *Baychimo*. To have so many confirmed sightings of a ship that sailed alone for thirty-eight years is nothing short of remarkable and we can only hope that one day soon the first images of this Arctic wonder are seen in the latest expeditions. For that we wish them all the luck in the world.

Chapter 30

Rawalpindi

The two world wars saw an increase in merchant vessels being armed in order to tackle the growing threat of German raiders and U-boats, in 1915, the Q-ships were everyday cargo ships that had a hidden gun and, when attacked on the surface by a submarine, the crew would simply collapse a false bulkhead on the upper deck and the hidden gun would emerge to retaliate. While the Q-ships themselves were not actually that successful in sinking submarines, that did not stop merchant ships becoming armed against the enemy.

By the outbreak of the Second World War these ships were known as Armed Merchant Cruisers and given the prefix HMS when fitted with these weapons. This could be anything from anti-aircraft guns to much larger surface-to-surface guns. It wouldn't be able to win a massive fight against a raider the size of a battleship, but it at least gave the ship a fighting chance against something a lot smaller or the ability to open fire on aircraft. At the worst they could give the enemy a bloody nose and send them packing.

One of these AMCs was the former P&O liner *Rawalpindi*, built in Greenock by Harland & Wolff in 1925. Over 16,000 gross tons, at 548 feet long, this two-funnel liner could carry around 600 passengers in two classes and would operate between London and India on a regular basis.

As war loomed, the *Rawalpindi* was requisitioned by the Admiralty just over a week before the official declaration. They knew that preparations had to be made and so she was fitted out as an AMC with eight 6-inch guns and a further two 3-inch guns. The fixtures and fittings that made her a luxury liner were all stripped in the dockyard, the hull was repainted in the dull grey of a warship and by the time she was ready to sail again she was flying the white ensign of the Royal Navy and had been turned into a single-funnel vessel.

Being taken off the luxury runs to India, the ship found herself on a patrol around the coast of Iceland where she located a German tanker, the

Gonzenheim, just days later, forcing the German crew to scuttle their ship before it could be taken.

The ship continued her patrol and on 23 November found herself off the Faroe Islands when, at around midday, two large warships were seen heading towards its position. These were the German battleships *Scharnhorst* and *Gneisenau*, although at the time it was believed that one of them was the 'pocket battleship' *Deutschland*. Quickly, they radioed the positions of the two ships back to Britain and turned to flee. There was no way that they could outrun the Germans, but they might be able to get within range of friendly units in time for them to get support. But, by 1600 hours that afternoon, it was clear that the ship was in range of the German guns. With no chance of running away anymore, Captain Edward Coverley Kennedy (father of Ludovic Kennedy) chose to fight the two ships. It was obvious that they could not escape the wrath of the German ships and so the *Rawalpindi* turned towards them and opened fire. In the meantime, her messages had been received and British warships were speeding towards the scene as fast as possible in the hope that they would not be too late. *Scharnhorst* and *Gneisenau* knew this would only be a matter of time but, within minutes, it was clearly not going to be an even fight and the chances of this lasting long enough for British ships to close in was diminishing.

The AMC had no real chance of doing any significant damage to the battleships. One shot from the *Rawalpindi* hit the *Scharnhorst*, causing very slight damage but the two warships closed in and pounded *Rawalpindi* with gunfire. Fires broke out everywhere, first taking out the ship's radio equipment and bridge.

The small-calibre guns were no match and before too long the gun crews were dead and the weapons unusable. Explosions continued as the warships' excellent gunnery skills destroyed the ship bit by bit. The lifeboats seemed to be all destroyed except a few, one of them being washed over the side as the ship listed.

It was just forty minutes from the start of the battle before they ceased fire. The blazing inferno on the AMC was left to just drift away, it being another two more hours to the *Rawalpindi* finally sinking, fires and explosions ending the life of a ship that had started out with so much to give and had heroically taken on two of Germany's finest battleships. She had no hope of winning, but to go down fighting like that took courage and for that her captain was posthumously Mentioned in Despatches.

That day 275 were killed on board the AMC. Twenty-seven survivors were picked up by the Germans with a further eleven found later by another converted liner, the AMC HMS *Chitral*, shivering in the cold lifeboat in the cruel Arctic conditions. *Chitral* brought the few survivors onboard and brought them back to Britain, all that was left of HMS *Rawalpindi* and almost 300 people. The two German warships made their escape and arrived back in Germany to a heroes' welcome.

The bravery of the crew of the *Rawalpindi* was a start to the war that nobody wanted to see, but it did bring home to people reading the story in the papers just how bad the situation must have been for them to sacrifice themselves like that. What would have been the outcome if they had surrendered? Would hundreds of people have been saved or would the two ships have carried on until she was sunk anyway?

The story of this ship went down in history, even more so when the captain's son, Ludovic Kennedy, published his biography of his own time with the Navy, which included being involved in the hunt for the *Bismarck* . Later he became a TV broadcaster and journalist. At the time of his father's death, Ludovic was 20 years old.

The wreck of the *Rawalpindi* has never been found, the waters around where she sank littered with shipwrecks of the convoys that would fall victim to the German navy over the next five years. Thanks to the reaction of the captain of the ship that day, the name of this vessel will forever be remembered as an action that not only surprised their foe but made everyone else on board the armed merchant cruisers sit up and listen.

Chapter 31

Jervis Bay and *San Demetrio*

T he convoy system during the wars seemed to alleviate a lot of the risk when it came to avoiding enemy craft such as surface raiders and U-boats, but for one convoy in particular there were two ships that stood out more than the others and for very different reasons.

Convoy HX84 was bound from Halifax, Nova Scotia to the UK, thirty-eight vessels in total, sailing on 28 October 1940 with two Canadian destroyers escorting them outside Canadian waters. After that it was up to the AMC HMS *Jervis Bay* to provide protection. *Jervis Bay* was a cargo liner built to cater for the Australian emigrant service and had been constructed at Barrow-in-Furness and launched in January 1922. At 549 feet long she was weighing in at just over 14,000 tons and could take at first over 700 third-class passengers but only twelve first-class, this was all changed during a conversion to a one-class passenger ship in 1931 when her total only came to 270 passengers, although this could be doubled by the addition of some temporary cabins if needed.

In 1939, like many other ships of that era, *Jervis Bay* was requisitioned by the Admiralty and fitted out as an armed merchant cruiser, with seven 6-inch guns fitted to her upper decks, and space on board for 255 crew. Looking at the situation with the convoys at this time, *Jervis Bay* stood no chance against an attack if all they had to offer was seven guns to protect thirty-eight ships.

One of these ships requiring protection was the very precious *San Demetrio*, a tanker that was loaded with aviation fuel and much needed for the war effort in Britain. Owned by the Eagle Oil & Shipping Co., she had been launched from her Scotstoun builders in 1938 and measured 463 feet long and was just over 8,000 gross tons. For personal protection, *San Demetrio* also had a few light guns on board, but those would be only useful for close range or anti-aircraft work.

The tanker had loaded her cargo in Aruba, before heading to join the convoy from Halifax. With the Canadian destroyers bidding their farewell, the convoy was alone and now making the perilous journey across the Atlantic.

On board *Jervis Bay* was Captain Edward Stephen Fogarty Fegen, a veteran of thirty-five years in the Royal Navy and already a recipient of the Sea Gallantry Medal for a daring rescue during the First World War. Aged 49, he was the sole carer for HX84 and on 5 November 1940 Fegen found himself on the receiving end of a seaborne emergency.

The German 'pocket battleship' *Admiral Scheer* had located the convoy and opened fire on the ships. Several vessels took direct hits, but the actions of the *Jervis Bay* left everybody in shock. Fegen turned his ship around and headed straight for the German raider, opening fire on the cruiser and causing a distraction long enough for the rest of the convoy to escape.

For twenty-four minutes the AMC took hit after hit, huge explosions and fire ripping into the ship, the convoy being ordered to scatter. None of *Jervis Bay*'s shots hit the *Admiral Scheer*, but still the ship kept on coming. The AMC was fully ablaze, her forward guns out of action, many of her crew dead. Fegen himself had taken a hit and lost an arm before giving the order to abandon ship. *Jervis Bay* went down with 189 souls, including Fegen.

The efforts of Captain Fegen and his crew to save the convoy did not go unnoticed. He was awarded a posthumous Victoria Cross.

With *Jervis Bay* sunk, the *Admiral Scheer* turned her attention to the rest of the convoy, although there were many fewer to fire upon now with it having scattered in every direction. One of the ships was the *San Demetrio* with her cargo of fuel which took a direct hit early on in the action and was soon on fire.

Knowing that the ship was carrying such a highly flammable cargo, the crew realised that they needed to get off the vessel as soon as possible. Three lifeboats left the ship and left the drifting tanker to burn and sink.

Two lifeboats containing the captain and twenty-five others were picked up safely but the third lifeboat with sixteen others was not faring so well. Second Officer Arthur Hawkins and Chief Engineer Charles Pollard were among those who were enduring pure hell at sea in freezing conditions and were exhausted through rowing and having the cold winds drain their energy. After twenty-four hours a ship was sighted but, to their dismay, they found it was the *San Demetrio*, still burning and still drifting.

After much discussion amongst themselves, the crew re-boarded the stricken tanker the following day, 7 November. They had more chance of survival if they went back onboard than if they were exposed in the open lifeboat to the elements. As soon as they got back on they put every effort into fighting the fire and keeping the ship afloat. After all it had lasted so long without blowing up and sinking, so there was a fighting chance she could still be saved.

The battle to save *San Demetrio* was a huge task. Not only were the fires extinguished but the chief engineer managed to get one of the engines working again. Setting up makeshift telegraph lights and repairing the steering gear, the tanker slowly made her way to Britain. Incredibly she was not attacked again.

It was seven days later that the *San Demetrio* shocked everyone by turning up unannounced off the coast of Ireland, a tug being told to go away due to the fact that the crew would now be entitled to salvage pay. With an entire tanker full of fuel, the rules stated that if a ship was abandoned and re-boarded without the captain in charge then those boarding were entitled to salvage money.

On 16 November 1940 the ship arrived in the Clyde, blackened and battered but only having lost about 200 tons of fuel. The crew had painted 'SOS' on the superstructure midships and what little food they had was being rationed, but the journey was over and they had arrived home to cheers. Second Officer Hawkins was presented with the ship's Red Ensign and appointed OBE for gallantry. The chief engineer was awarded Lloyds War Medal for Bravery at Sea.

The heroic efforts to save the ship was made into a film before the war had even ended. *San Demetrio London* was released in 1943 and was a success and morale booster to those who had the patriotic feel during what were some very dark days for the Allies.

But the tanker herself was repaired and put back into service. On 14 March 1942 *San Demetrio* sailed from Maryland, USA bound for the UK, joining a Halifax convoy with 4,000 tons of alcohol and 7,000 tons of aviation spirit. Just three days later the German submarine *U-404* attacked the convoy and *San Demetrio* was hit by torpedoes and went down. Nineteen crew died and thirty-two were later rescued in lifeboats.

So ended the career of the *San Demetrio*, a ship that had a miraculous tale of survival, much like the later *Ohio* on the Malta convoys. It was incredible that two ships with such tales could be in the same convoy, but the story of the *Jervis Bay* and *San Demetrio* have now gone down in history as lost ships, but with crews who did something quite extraordinary in the face of overwhelming odds and yet still stared death in the face.

Chapter 32

Marine Sulphur Queen

Any book about the Bermuda Triangle in the modern day has a number of the top ships that have gone missing in this area, but the story of the *Marine Sulphur Queen* is near the top of that list as being one that supposedly vanished and was never seen again. The only flaw to this otherwise perfect mystery is the fact that parts of her were actually found with wreckage picked up which not only confirmed it to be from the ship but it literally spelled out the name.

The 504-foot-long tanker was launched in Pennsylvania in 1944 as the *Esso New Haven* and was 10,642 gross tons, an oil-carrying vessel that was operated by a crew of thirty-nine and later converted to carry molten sulphur, for which she had a change of name in 1960 to *Marine Sulphur Queen*.

To convert the ship to her new role the insides had to be remodelled with the construction of a new tank and the removal of all inner bulkheads that would no longer be used. She set sail on 2 February 1963 from Beaumont in Texas with a cargo of 15,260 tons of sulphur, bound for Norfolk, Virginia.

There were several incidents that had befallen the ship and a later investigation would be shocked to hear that there were so many fires on board the vessel around the tank that the crew didn't even sound the alarm in the end. On one occasion, the ship made a journey into New Jersey, offloaded her cargo and then set sail again with a fire onboard the entire time. Another aspect to these incidents was that when the sulphur fire was extinguished it would dribble around the equipment and solidify, causing electrical components to short out. Looking at where this was taking place highlighted many cracks in the structure of the ship.

In January *Marine Sulphur Queen* was due into dry dock but the owners postponed it due to the fact that the cargo schedules would be late. So bad was the ship that the crew compared it to nothing more than a dustbin at sea. These tankers needed the dry dock inspections as they had a fatal flaw of having the keel splitting at a certain weak point; this had occurred on more than one occasion on other tankers of the same classes. Crew members also highlighted that the *Marine Sulphur Queen* was covered in corrosion and a lot of the equipment on board did not function correctly.

With the tanker having the reputation of being a ship that people just didn't want to be onboard, she still managed to carry a full complement of crew. Two days out of Texas, the ship radioed in that she was in a position off the coast of Florida.

That was the last anybody ever heard of the *Marine Sulphur Queen*. It was two days later that the vessel was officially listed as missing when she failed to arrive at the destination. The fact that the ship had sailed into a storm during this period rang alarm bells, especially amongst those who already knew its state.

A search was launched for the missing ship and went on for a total of nineteen days. Random pieces of wreckage were soon found floating in the sea confirming that the worst had happened. The US Coast Guard scoured the seas and, on 20 February, a nearby US Naval vessel on exercise found part of the ship's name board, a life ring, a lifejacket and various other parts identified as coming from the missing ship. But no more was found and there was no sign of her crew of thirty-nine.

An inquiry was launched into what could have possibly gone wrong and this is where the evidence was heard into the state of the ship that had now taken so many people to their watery graves. Although an exact cause of the loss of the *Marine Sulphur Queen* could not be determined for certain, it was thought that a number of possibilities could have occurred, but none in particular was pinpointed.

An onboard explosion of the cargo would explain the shattered wreckage, the failure of the hull would fit the pattern of ships of that class that had suffered the same problems. Capsizing due to bad weather was a possibility and a steam explosion caused by a rapid filling of a void space with water were the another two of the four top probabilities but, based on very little evidence, they could each be as likely as they were unlikely. To ensure that this tragedy would not be repeated, the investigation by the Coast Guard recommended that no other tankers of that nature would be allowed to be converted to carry sulphur.

The wives of several crew members were outraged at the condition the ship was allowed to be in and challenged the owners by threatening legal action. A later court case found the owners liable for the state of the ship and awarded damages to the families of the missing crew, although even this only went so far, due to the fact that the causes of death and reason for sinking were both undetermined.

Due to the fact that the ship and the entire crew remained missing, the ship started becoming a 'conspiracy' for those who were fans of the Bermuda Triangle theory. While omitting the fact that wreckage was located on the surface, it now joins many other ships that have vanished without trace to be victims of the Triangle. All very well for those trying to make something of a sea mystery, but the truth is that the ship was unfit to go to sea, had a highly flammable cargo and had sailed into a storm. It was only a matter of time before those elements would have at least seriously damaged the ship, let alone sink it.

But still the Triangle keeps coming up in posts about this ship; every kind of supernatural explanation and conspiracy theory is discussed when the truth would actually be easier to find just by reading the newspapers.

Like many of these ships tarred with the Triangle brush, the wreck of the *Marine Sulphur Queen* has not been found and has most likely not been looked for on the seabed. Only when we see what condition the wreck is in may we decide the true cause of this ship's sinking.

Until then we are blessed with the comical 'news2' reports that the tanker had been found in the middle of a Libyan desert with 'Soviet cigarette butts' on board. How a ship of that size got there and just happened to leave wreckage in the waters off Florida is not explained.

But until the wreck is finally located, the mystery of what really happened to the *Marine Sulphur Queen* will occupy the pages of the books of the unexplained, the Bermuda Triangle enthusiasts and those who want to glorify the thirty-nine missing sailors as a supernatural event. They may be disappointed to eventually find out that simple negligence on a ship barely fit to sail would be the true cause.

Chapter 33

The Triple Trawler Tragedy

On 20 May 2022 the city of Hull in East Yorkshire came together to pay their respects at the funeral of a woman who had been part of a huge trawler safety campaign in the 1960s. Yvonne Blenkinsop was the last of the 'headscarf revolutionaries', a group of four fishermen's wives who fought the fishing industry and won against overwhelming odds for better safety on the trawlers that would depart from Hull on a dangerous Arctic voyage, many of them never to be seen again.

It was in the early months of 1968 that the *Hull Daily Mail* ran with headlines featuring these four women – Yvonne together with Lillian Bilocca, Christine Smallbone and Mary Denness – who were protesting angrily at the loss of three trawlers in such a short space of time and that ships were still departing the docks at St Andrew's Quay without a working radio, or with the captain being the only one able to operate the radio and therefore doing two jobs at once. With conditions already horrendous for the crews of around twenty per ship, it was all too often that a ship would have a man overboard, or even worse the ship itself would be sunk in stormy seas.

On 10 January 1968 two of those trawlers left the docks on the same day, the *St Romanus* and *Kingston Peridot*, bound for the icy fishing grounds of the Arctic Circle. It was standard practice to radio the owners on a daily basis to give an update on where the vessel was operating, but many of the ships would not do this in case a rival sneaked in and took all their fish from right under their noses. *St Romanus* did a radio-telephone message the same evening and headed north. Nobody worried that they had not had any further contact from the ship. Both trawlers had twenty crew members on board and were built for the conditions that they would be experiencing, so few people worried when the ships went into radio silence.

On the 20th, the *Ross Cleveland* sailed from the same dock with twenty crewmen on board. However, one of the crew members became ill and the ship headed towards Iceland to send him ashore to receive treatment.

Then, on the 26th, over two weeks after the *St Romanus* and *Kingston Peridot* had sailed, there came some worrying news. The *Kingston Peridot* had been working off the north-east coast of Iceland in terrible weather and was in contact with another nearby vessel via radio. She told them that a huge build-up of ice on the upper decks was causing major issues and their intention was to head east as soon as possible to where the others were. That was the last time anyone heard from the *Kingston Peridot*.

The same day the owners tried to contact the *St Romanus* for an update. No matter how many times they tried, they could not raise the trawler on the airwaves. What was worse was that news soon filtered through that, almost two weeks previously, on the 13th, a life raft had been located and had been confirmed as coming from the *St Romanus*. This meant that *St Romanus* had been missing for that length of time and not a soul had been searching for her.

The newspapers were hungry for details of what was happening. The search for the missing *St Romanus* and her twenty crew had shocked the tightly-knit fishing community and everyone was eager to hear about the search that had been launched for the ship, hoping and praying that a miracle would happen and it would be found safe, or that survivors would be picked up. But hope faded as the days passed with no news.

On 30 January 1968 Hull was in mourning for the crew of *St Romanus* when more shocking news greeted them. A life raft had washed ashore along with other debris, but this was not from *St Romanus* – it was from the *Kingston Peridot*. All indications suggested that the vessel had gone down on the 27th, a full three days earlier. With this news of two ships and forty people missing, the city once again went into shock.

A few days later, on 3 February, the *Ross Cleveland* sailed from Iceland after landing her sick crewman ashore. Heading to a sheltered area on the north-west coast of the island, she would join several other trawlers that had gathered to wait for the storm to pass. This wasn't an average storm, for any bad weather in that area of the world would be ten times worse than anywhere else. The biting cold, snow and blizzard conditions, ice on deck and crashing waves that would freeze in all crevices, were just some of the hazards they faced. The following day, the captain of the *Ross Cleveland* moved the vessel to what he believed would be a safer area, but the crew were struggling to control the ship which was becoming overwhelmed by the huge amounts of ice on deck that were making her top heavy.

The captain of the *Ross Cleveland* sent a radio message out as a final desperate call so that everyone in the area would know that they were in trouble and capsizing. Then it was silence. Ships attempted to head to the scene, but their own fight against the storm was getting them nowhere, two other ships sinking in this storm.

Unlike the *St Romanus* and *Kingston Peridot*, the news of the *Ross Cleveland* sinking reached Hull the day after and a search and rescue operation was already in full swing, not that anybody expected to find anything like the other two. But, incredibly, a miracle did happen. Harry Eddom, the mate of the *Ross Cleveland*, had been on the upper deck at the time of the capsizing and had managed to get into a life raft which had been washed ashore in Iceland.

He staggered to shelter at a summer house where he found shelter from the wind by standing behind the building. The following morning, a young boy found him and led him to his father, where he was cared for until he could be rescued. This sparked a media circus as the newspapers bombarded him with interview requests, one even flying his family over to Iceland to meet him. Fights broke out between rival reporters and hospital staff.

The city of Hull went from shock and mourning to anger. Fisherman's wife Lillian Bilocca got together with the three other women and became known as the Headscarf Revolutionaries. They had already decided that nobody was listening to their pleas to make the trawlers safer, so direct action had to be the way ahead. Starting with petitions and meetings, this soon grew into full-blown confrontation with the trawler owners when they marched to the dockside and shouted at the trawlers leaving port, questioning if they were safe – did they have a radioman on board? Life rafts? Enough people?

Police held back the protestors attempting to jump on board and the fight for safety regulations went to parliament, as well as the front pages of the papers. But it wasn't without sacrifice, the tabloids ridiculing the women and many fishermen showing their own anger at these people who should not interfere with 'men's work' and even received death threats. But their persistence paid off and soon the law was changed to ensure that trawler safety was of paramount importance. The Hull Headscarf Revolutionaries changed everything, but only after their campaign was highlighted by the loss of three trawlers and fifty-eight lives. The Triple Trawler Tragedy is today commemorated in several places across Hull with memorial ceremonies taking place on the anniversaries and plaques to commemorate not only the sunken ships but also of the monumental efforts by the campaigners.

Of the three sunken ships, one of them has been located. In the summer of 2002, a BBC TV crew located the *Ross Cleveland* wreck and confirmed that the cause of the sinking was a build-up of ice on the upper decks. The ghostly images of the wreck included the name on the bow, a final confirmation of this wreck's identity.

For the *St Romanus* and *Kingston Peridot*, with the ships not actually being missed for such a long time before being reported, their wrecks still remain undiscovered.

Chapter 34

Berge Vanga and *Berge Istra*

The largest ships to regularly plough the world's oceans are without doubt the monsters that are the bulk carriers and oil tankers. They are massive ships designed to carry 100,000-ton cargoes with ease, slowly moving from port to port delivering their expensive fuels and materials, crewed by only a handful of people, keeping costs down and profits up. But it is when these ships meet with an accident that the role of the bulker is highlighted and, as the ships have got larger, the disasters have been greater.

In 1980 the bulk carrier *Derbyshire* went missing in the South China Sea during a typhoon. It would be a deep-sea expedition in 1994 that eventually located the wreck in seven large sections on the seabed. Her sister ship had grounded and split open at a point previously highlighted as a weak area in the vessel. Other vessels suffered similar fates, the seas breaking the backs of ships and leaving them sliced in half and floating alone. On one occasion the crew of the *Flare* abandoned ship and were pleased to see a ship coming towards them to rescue them, only to then find it was the bow half of their own ship drifting.

So, this next pair of shipwrecks come as a bit of a mystery in several ways. In the years when bulk carriers were still new, any loss of a ship of that size would cause concern, especially if the same thing happened twice.

The *Berge Istra* was an ore-bulk-oil carrier built in Yugoslavia in 1972 for the Norwegian shipping company Bergesen d.y. and was 227,550 tonnes deadweight. At over 1,000-feet long, her main role was taking a variety of iron ore and oil from ports around the Pacific regions and over to South America. It was on one of those journeys that something happened to her when the ship was only three years old.

At the end of December 1975, she was scheduled to carry ore from Brazil to Japan, before heading to the Persian Gulf and Europe with oil, a simple change over that had been done often in the past. She arrived in the Brazilian port of Tubarao, filled up with the iron ore and sailed without any problems, heading to the Japanese port of Kimitsu. On 30 December she made her last contact with the outside world and was never heard from again.

It would be over a week before the ship was reported missing. On 7 January 1976 a search and rescue operation was launched with no sign of the huge ship or what could have happened to her. After nine days, the search was called off and the ship listed as most likely having sunk, reasons unknown.

But just forty-eight hours later, on 18 January, a Japanese fishing vessel came across a raft with two Spanish crew members from the *Berge Istra*. They had been stranded at sea for twenty days and all rescue operations had missed them completely. They confirmed that the ship had suffered three major explosions and broke in two around 550 miles south-east of Mindanao in the Philippines. Thirty of their shipmates had not been so fortunate.

The sinking of the *Berge Istra* was very similar to a disaster that occurred just two years previously when the oil tanker *Golar Patricia*, also owned by a Norwegian company, suddenly suffered three explosions and broke in two mid-Atlantic. In this case, everybody except one person managed to survive. This highlighted the dangers of these ships and questions began to be raised as to what was going wrong with vessels of that size, and if there was anything that could be done to find out what was causing the blasts. *Golar Patricia* was the largest ship ever lost at the time. That record was overtaken by *Berge Istra*.

Although a ship that size shouldn't just vanish, let alone randomly blow up and split in two, what happened after has caused even more confusion over the years, leading to this shipwreck becoming a talking point and a cue for conspiracies to start.

First of all, let's look at another ship owned by the same company, the sister ship to *Berge Istra*, the *Berge Vanga*. She was built in the same place as the *Berge Istra*, was slightly heavier deadweight at 227,912 tonnes and designed to do the same job in the same ports around Brazil and Japan. So, when contact was lost with this ship on 29 October 1979, alarm bells started to ring. There were forty people on board and to lose a second ship of this magnitude in just under four years was unheard of. Once again, a huge search operation was launched to hunt for the missing ship, with the hope that the crew had managed to escape in time should a disaster have occurred.

Nothing was found but a little bit of debris floating on the surface, most likely miles away from where the ship had gone down. Not a single survivor was found and, eventually, the search was called off. Once more, a ship of significant size had gone down without anyone even noticing.

With two huge ships vanishing, this alone would have been enough to start a discussion amongst those suspecting something was seriously amiss. But then the hearings were started in complete secrecy. The owners refused to talk about the loss of the two ships and any evidence was kept under wraps.

The main cause of the loss of the ships was only a theory: that a build-up of vapours from oil residue had ignited causing a catastrophic explosion that had wrecked the ships quite suddenly. The two survivors from *Berge Istra* were the only eyewitnesses to what had happened and their stories are sought after from people who want answers even today.

One thing that the loss of the two ships did change was that no more vessels were built that could transport both cargoes; instead, they were designed as either bulk carriers or oil tankers. Switching between the two depending on the voyage was no longer an option.

But the mysterious loss of the *Berge Istra* and *Berge Vanga* continue to be discussed. In the age of the internet, there is never an escape when people need information or want to discuss what they think went on, or why the secrecy? Despite an obvious wish for the subject to go away, this is most likely one of those sea mysteries that will still fascinate people for years to come, especially if one day the two wrecks are located on the seabed.

For *Berge Istra*, a book was released in 1989 telling of the exploits of the ship and the survivors but, in 2020, a new documentary was released with exclusive interviews with them and the story of what is known about the loss of the ship today, once again putting the story of the vessels into the limelight.

After the *Derbyshire* sank in 1980 it was said that she would be impossible to find. When the state of the wreck was broadcast to the world it became obvious that questions needed to be asked. It may only be a matter of time before the same questions are asked again in relation to these two Norwegian behemoths.

Chapter 35

Marques

The most beautiful ships ever to grace the oceans have always been the sailing vessels, with a certain flair above all others which put clippers like the *Cutty Sark* and barques such as the *Marques* at the forefront of the photographer's lens. Events like the 1984 Tall Ships Race was one period that attracted thousands of ship enthusiasts. By the time the 67-year-old *Marques* joined this competition, she had already had a long and eventful life sailing the seas. Built in Valencia in Spain, she was 120-feet long and weighed in at around 300 tons, originally built as a brig and used as a cargo vessel to transport supplies around the Mediterranean ports.

Suffering damage during the Second World War she was repaired and, unfortunately, neglected until she was in a very bad condition. In 1971 she was purchased by a man from the UK, Robin Cecil-Wright, who brought the ship into Southampton. She soon found herself being restored lovingly and used in TV shows and films, most notably *The Onedin Line*, a very popular series that ran for several years.

Six years after being saved, a Mr Mark Litchfield bought a half share of the vessel which soon found herself back on the TV screens starring as HMS *Beagle*, the ship in which Charles Darwin sailed the oceans and made himself a household name. Starring Malcolm Stoddard as Darwin, the series ran on for seven episodes in 1978 with *Marques* being the star of the show.

In 1983 the ship sailed from Plymouth to carry out charter tours in the hotter climates of the West Indies region and by the summer of the following year was at the Cutty Sark Tall Ships Race, winning first prize in the first leg from Puerto Rico to Bermuda. On the second part, from Hamilton to Halifax, Nova Scotia, the *Marques* sailed on 2 June with high hopes. One of forty-two ships from twenty countries, her twenty-eight crew got to work harder than ever in the hope that the name of this ship would continue to stay at the top of the leader board.

In the early morning of 2 June the ship was in rough weather. Gale force winds battered the ship, although the crew believed they were already through the worst of it when the skies were seen to be clearing, until suddenly she was slammed onto her starboard side unexpectedly. This could have been a rogue wave combined with a squall, but the result was catastrophic as, within seconds, she was flooding down below with the main hatch already allowing tons of water in. Her crew barely stood a chance at getting out, the *Marques* rolling over in the storm and sinking within a minute.

At around 0700 a nearby schooner sighted a distress signal and raised the alarm. Another, the *Zawisza Czarny*, saw a life raft in the water that had been released as the ship had gone down. Nine people had managed to struggle into the raft and were taken on board the Polish ship; the other nineteen crew were missing. In the end, only one body was ever recovered.

A rescue operation was launched by the Coast Guard and US Navy after the *Zawisza Czarny* alerted them, every ship nearby scouring the seas for the missing crew but with no luck. The rest of the life-saving rafts and dinghies were found floating empty on the Atlantic swell. Debris from the lost barque floated around, the only mark that any ship had been there and all that was left of nineteen lives.

Back in Britain an inquiry was opened to determine the cause of the sinking of the *Marques* over a year after the disaster, with testimony being given by Robin Cecil-Wright. He said that the ship had actually sprung a leak on several occasions in the 1970s during the filming of the Darwin TV show, although the damaged planks in that case were all replaced.

In the end the disaster was blamed on the weather, although stability of the vessel has raised its head in several reports, and a book on the loss of several tall ships. What was a tragic epilogue to the loss of this fine ship was a separate incident that occurred eleven years after the loss of the *Marques*.

On 30 May 1995 the historic 137-year-old brig *Maria Asumpta* was on a voyage off the south coast of England as part of her role as a sail-training vessel carrying sixteen people. That afternoon, the ship was crossing a stretch of land that was fairly hazardous and not recommended. The ship lost power suddenly and, within minutes, had grounded on nearby rocks, with water beginning to flood the holds below. The crew abandoned ship but three of them didn't make it and drowned.

The grounding of the *Maria Asumpta* made headlines, not least when it was found out who owned the vessel – *Marques*'s owners Robin Cecil-Wright and Mark Litchfield. Only this time Litchfield was actually on board the sinking ship and had been in charge of the vessel as the captain.

He was soon charged with manslaughter due to gross negligence and, after a trial where all the evidence into the sinking as well as highlighting the fact that he part-owned the lost *Marques*, a jury found him guilty and he was given a jail term of eighteen months.

The tragic thing about the sinkings of both *Marques* and the *Maria Asumpta* is that these ships were historic, photogenic vessels and had a long history between them. To have them still both sailing the seas was something of a novelty for vessels of their vintage especially, when considering the pounding they take in rough weather.

But when both went down the world lost two great ships and twenty-two people. But they were not the first sailing ships to be sunk and most likely won't be the last. In 2007, the *Cutty Sark* burning in her dry dock in Greenwich was both a tragic sight and led to an incredible restoration project that got the ship back to her original state and once again open to the public. As time goes on, we have to look after these relics of the sea before they are all lost to history.

While the *Maria Asumpta* was on the rocks against the land, the wreck of the *Marques* is today somewhere off the coast of the Caribbean islands, waiting for the day when underwater cameras revive her story.

Chapter 36
Andrea Gail

One of the most heart-wrenching films to have come out in the early part of the twenty-first century, which told a true story about man against the sea, was the blockbuster Hollywood movie *The Perfect Storm*. Based on the eponymous book by Sebastian Junger, it told the tale about a group of six fishermen who sailed out of port to be met by the worst that nature could throw at them. Although it was heavily dramatised due to the fact that we know very little about what really went on, it still brings home just how much risk the humble fisherman takes when taking a small boat to sea in weather that would make even the strongest of stomachs churn.

The *Andrea Gail*, a 13-year-old steel-hulled fishing vessel of 57.9 feet in length and 92 gross tons, regularly fished out of her home port of Gloucester, Massachusetts, and in October 1991 it was just another routine journey back out to the Grand Banks fishing grounds to make a living. Frank 'Billy' Tyne was the skipper, a man who was well respected by the crews of the boats that regularly sailed out of the harbour and most of those who served under him. Before the journey, the boat crews would spend some of their hard-earned cash at the local bar on the edge of the harbour, a place called The Crow's Nest, where everybody knew everybody else and a sudden loss of a vessel would hit the area hard.

The *Andrea Gail* was not a huge ship. Her green hull and sharp bow cutting through the waves was not remarkable either, one of several near identical swordfishing boats that would head out for weeks at a time in the hope of getting the big catch that would net them a tidy profit. Living on board any fishing vessel of this size was cramped at the best of times, but these men were used to it and they had to take the rough with the smooth if they wanted a good wage.

Life at sea on this fishing vessel was hard work. A crew member could be up most of the night depending on what was required from him and, to make matters worse, if the catch was not good enough then the pay suffered. If you don't catch enough, you don't get paid enough. It was all down to what you could get at the end when the catch was landed, weighed and sold. Once this was completed, it was back out again at the next opportunity, if you could hack it of course; for some it was not the life for them.

Andrea Gail sailed off on her regular voyage on 21 September 1991, with enough supplies and fuel to last around six-to-seven weeks, her sister vessel *Hannah Boden* close by and in radio contact; the two captains were good friends as well as fishing rivals. With five crew on board as well as Captain Tyne, there was no reason to suggest that this voyage would be any different from the countless others. It was only due to bad luck with the swordfish stocks that the skipper made the decision to head east towards the Flemish Cap, well out of their usual hunting grounds. But, again, there was nothing to say that the voyage would not be successful and that they return home with a hefty pay cheque.

That is until it was noted at the weather stations around the eastern seaboard of the United States that not one but three tropical storms were coming in from different angles. As the days went by those storms grew stronger until, on 28 October, the unthinkable happened – they collided. A colossal storm was in full swing across the coast, the waves were around sixty-feet high out at sea causing huge container ships to struggle to keep on course. Yachts had to have rescue helicopters airlift their crews to safety and, in the middle of all this, the *Andrea Gail* battled the seas in an attempt to get home. The *Hannah Boden* received a radio message from *Andrea Gail* that same day saying that the boat was struggling in thirty-foot high seas and up to 80 knots of wind. Further contact between the two vessels was not successful and several attempts by the owners to raise her on the radio came to nothing.

But that was the last anyone ever heard from the *Andrea Gail*. Once the vessel had been reported as overdue, a rescue operation was launched on the 31st and dozens of United States Coast Guard ships and aircraft combed the Atlantic for ten days. During this time, small amounts of wreckage were found, bearing what looked like the vessel's initials, as well as the emergency beacon later found to be registered to the boat, but the six crew were never found and nor was the *Andrea Gail* herself. Her loss was investigated by the Coast Guard but, with a lack of evidence, the vessel was simply classed as 'missing' and all six crew 'missing and presumed dead'

The port of Gloucester went into mourning. The crews knowing each other and drinking in the same den was really brought home as the families wept at a memorial service. Six more names were added to the fishermen's memorial. They were not the first and have certainly not been the last. But the name of this vessel lived on with the release of Junger's book in 1997 where an immense amount of research pieced together the final days of Tyne and his crew in their battle for survival against the elements. The book was a huge success and, a few years later, in 2000, came the movie that brought the *Andrea Gail* and her crew into the limelight. With A-list celebrities such as George Clooney playing the skipper, along with Mark Wahlberg and John C. Reilly as two of the crew members, it was always going to be a cinema sell out. The film was released and became a tear-jerking success, invoking a new-found respect in many people for the simple fishermen of the world who ply the seas while the rest of us sleep. Thanks to the hard work of this author, and his dedication to bring the story to print, the name of the *Andrea Gail* will now live on in more than just names stamped onto a memorial plaque.

But this was not the end of the story, for 2005 saw famous author Clive Cussler search for the wreck of the *Andrea Gail* with his team of divers. Trawling over the probable area of the wreck they came up with nothing, but it did make a fascinating documentary for the TV series *The Sea Hunters* which aired that year.

So, a regular fishing vessel that was given celebrity status remains officially missing at sea, as do her six crew. Even if the book and film had not been made, the names of Billy Tyne, Alfred Pierre, Bobby Shatford, Michael Moran, Dale Murphy and David Sullivan are forever on the memorial and forever remembered by those who mourn them more than anyone else – their close families and friends.

Chapter 37

München

I t is surprising that huge ships still go missing in the modern day, but in 1978 the cargo ship *München* joined that list of shipwrecks with no explanation and no clue as to where it went down. Launched on 12 May 1972, she was a ship known as a LASH carrier, or Lighter Aboard Ship, a vessel designed to transport smaller vessels such as lighters (a type of barge). These barges are meant for inland waterways but when they require movement across open seas it is neither safe nor practical simply to tow them across water to their new place of work. Built in Belgium, she was a German vessel owned by Hapag-Lloyd and carried out her maiden voyage in October 1972. With a crew of twenty-eight hands, she was 37,134 gross tons and 858 feet long, a huge ship. Her first voyage took a total of thirty-five days.

On 7 December 1978, under the command of Captain Johann Danekamp, she sailed from Bremerhaven carrying a cargo of steel products within eighty-three lighters and a nuclear reactor vessel heading to Combustion Engineering Inc. Her aim was to transit the Atlantic to her destination of Savannah, Georgia, where she would then offload her cargo on what would be her sixty-second voyage.

On this trip, though, there was a fierce storm that had been battering the North Atlantic for several weeks, but with *München* being so big, and being designed to weather such a storm, the ship carried on as normal and sailed right into the bad weather. A voyage like this was nothing new for the crew of this enormous vessel.

Just after midnight on 12 December, one of the crew members, radio operator Jorg Ernst, was talking to his friend aboard the cruise ship *Caribe* over 2,000 miles away, a conversation that was overheard. He spoke of bad weather and the ship having taken some damage along the way, his position also being given out, although the reception was too bad to make out most of what was being said. As this was not an official radio transmission and just chat between friends, this information was not relayed back to the ship's owners for several days. In any case, there seemed little to worry about since, although he reported damage to portholes, he signed off by saying 'see you soon'.

A few hours later, a distress call was picked up by a Greek freighter, which relayed it on to several other ships, that *München* was in trouble and talked about 'fifty degrees starboard', which could indicate that the ship had a severe list.

At 0443 (GMT), emergency signals were beginning to be received by numerous radio stations. Later that evening, a full search and rescue operation was in force, co-ordinated by the Cornwall Coastguard station at Land's End. The weather was horrendous and the winds were severely hampering any efforts to get a search underway, the RAF being called in to assist with the use of a Nimrod aircraft.

By the next day over twenty-four hours had passed since the *München* first transmitted a distress call and several aircraft had joined the search, along with several ships. Unreliable radio messages were being received which may or may not have come from the missing ship, but these were reported, as were the others. At the US Navy base at Rota, Spain, ten very weak Mayday calls were received that supposedly came from *München*, giving the callsign DEAT in Morse code and mentioning 'twenty-eight persons aboard'.

By then dozens of ships were searching for the *München*, including salvage tugs and sixteen aircraft based temporarily in the Azores. The storms were dropping slightly by the 14th but by then signals from an emergency buoy were being received. This usually means that the ship has gone down and released the beacon automatically; hopes that the ship was still afloat were not high.

This was confirmed later that day when a British cargo ship found an empty life raft and a German vessel located several of the *München*'s lighters that had floated free. An aircraft flew over several objects in the water on the 15th and a tug found a second life raft. The next day a third was found. All were unoccupied. Various other pieces of wreckage were found in the coming days, confirming that the ship had gone down and not one single person had managed to make it to a life raft. Given the state of the sea during the search, it was not surprising; only a few things designed to float had been located.

By the evening of 20 December 1978, the search for the *München* was officially called off, although the owners, along with the West German Government, carried on for another forty-eight hours supported by UK and US forces. The last remnants of the missing ship were found on 16 February 1979 when the car transporter *Don Carlos* found and salvaged a wrecked lifeboat.

With a ship of this size sinking, many questions were being asked as to what could have caused such a large vessel to founder in weather that it was designed to handle. When the lifeboat was examined, it highlighted some frightening facts, namely that the pins connecting it to the block had been bent back by a force of some extreme nature, while the fact that this lifeboat was almost seventy feet above sea level led to a conclusion that the nature of the storm had created some kind of monster rogue wave large enough to rip the lifeboat from the high decks and batter the ship so badly that she then sank.

Very little was known about rogue waves at the time of the loss of the *München*, but, as further investigation showed, it was possible for a wave of considerable size to exist in deep water areas. That a ship such as the *München* was hit by a wave of such force implies that there was a trough so large that the ship could plunge into it, with the upper decks vulnerable to any powerful force smashing the bow head on.

With no proof of any of this, other than what was recovered, we can only speculate what the crew had to endure in this period. It was obvious that the ship had been in distress for many hours and did not sink straightaway. Was it one bad wave that disabled her or did several more hit her in the coming hours? The investigation concluded that the ship had perhaps stayed afloat for around thirty hours after its first emergency call. We can only imagine how terrifying that must have been for the twenty-five men and three women who were on board.

Today it is estimated that the *München* gave her position a possible 100 miles away from where she actually was. Sailing into a storm of this magnitude may have damaged her long before any freak wave had put paid to her sailing days and the fact that none of the rafts were found occupied means that the ship had either lost all her survival equipment or the crew were unable to jump overboard and get into one safely. No bodies were ever recovered which could also mean that they were sheltering inside hoping for rescue when the ship finally went down.

The ship has since featured on several TV documentaries about rogue waves, more evidence of them being available today than there was over forty years before. A model of the *München* is on display at the German

Naval Memorial in Laboe, near Kiel, a cargo ship surrounded by the warships of the navy, but one which has caused modern-day controversy and too many questions.

Today the wreck remains undiscovered, with no plans to search for her.

Part V
Passenger Ships

Chapter 38

Arctic

It is incredible to think that a ship with hundreds of people onboard could still not be located over a century on, but these next chapters will show that neither size nor occupancy mean a thing when the sea shall have them.

In the early days of the steamship, the only way to convert the engine power to motion was by paddle-wheels mounted on the sides of a ship. Once this was proven, the building of bigger ships became possible while passenger numbers also grew. Such vessels were seaworthy and faster than the conventional sailing ships and attractive to owners. One such was built in New York in 1850: the SS *Arctic* was owned by the New York and Liverpool Mail Steamship Company, also known as the Collins Line.

She was 2,856 tons and 284 feet long when she started her maiden voyage on 26 October across the Atlantic to Liverpool. She was making excellent time and could regularly do a trans-ocean crossing in just nine to ten days which was great news for her owners who by now found that she had been nicknamed the 'clipper of the sea'.

By the end of 1853 she had already made a number of successful crossings but then met with a series of unfortunate incidents. On 23 November that year she grounded in Liverpool Bay and was later re-floated without incident, but just six months later, on 18 May 1854, she struck rocks off County Wexford in Ireland. Again, she was soon re-floated and brought back into port.

Four months later, 20 September, she was departing Liverpool, bound for New York with up to 300 passengers and around 150 crew. On board were close family of the owners of the ship, including Mary Ann Collins, wife of Edward Collins, the founder of the Collins Line.

The following day the *Arctic* passed southern Ireland and entered the Atlantic Ocean. Bringing the ship up to the maximum speed of 13 knots, she gracefully cruised the ocean and the passengers settled into their week at sea. The voyage was uneventful as were most of her other crossings and a week after sailing she was already approaching the Grand Banks of Newfoundland. Since the area had a reputation for fog, caused by the cold Labrador current meeting the warm Gulf Stream, ships were obliged to go as fast as possible through it to reduce time spent in poor visibility. However, applying this philosophy increased the risk of being involved in a collision with another ship.

At around midday on 27 September the ship was in fog as expected. Suddenly, out of the gloom, a steamship was taking shape heading right towards them. Despite attempts to avoid the oncoming ship the *Arctic* was struck on the starboard side, although to many it didn't seem as if the collision had actually been that bad. Some believed it to be a slight bump and nobody was panicking. In fact, passengers carried on going about their day, wondering what the bump was, yet not thinking much more of it.

However, the French ship *Vesta*, the vessel that had collided with the *Arctic*, was in a bad way. Her bow was smashed and seemed to be folded back. Panic was evident with around 200 people running around the upper deck. The crew of the *Arctic* began launching their lifeboats to assist with *Vesta*'s evacuation, but one of them pointed out that the *Arctic* herself had developed a list.

This was quite worrying, especially when it was found that parts of the *Vesta*'s bow were embedded in the hull of the *Arctic* and that the ship had been damaged, with her hull penetrated and open to the sea. What was now evident was that the design of the *Arctic* meant that there were no watertight bulkheads. The ship was completely open to the sea from bow to stern. The *Arctic* was sinking.

The liner's pumps tried to hold off the water but this would only allow so much to be pumped out before becoming overwhelmed. An attempt to staunch the holes in the hull with a sail came to naught when protruding jagged wreckage ripped the fabric. It then became apparent that the liner might actually make it closer to land with Cape Race but four hours away. So, the ship turned back towards land and went as fast as possible.

Unfortunately, within minutes, the *Arctic* rammed into one of the *Vesta*'s lifeboats, killing all onboard but one. In the meantime, water levels were rising and the decision was made to abandon ship. Boats were being launched, but it seemed to some that the boats did not have enough room for everybody on board so there was now a mad rush to get on board the lifeboats, causing chaos, while boats were being overturned, killing the people on board.

The crew continued to rush the boats in a desperate effort to get away. More boats were upended and those that were launched were only partly full when they got away. A group of engineers commandeered one boat, threatening anybody who came near it with a gun. Their excuse was that they were using it to try to plug the leaks, but everybody knew by this time that the *Arctic* was doomed.

One young crewman was ordered to fire the ship's signal cannon on the bow every minute to attract help. Stewart Holland, only a trainee engineer, continued doing this until the ship went down. He did not survive as the *Arctic*'s bow slipped beneath the waves, the hull going down by the stern until there was nothing left but a mass of wreckage, bodies and lifeboats.

It was only when two lifeboats made landfall at Broad Cove on 29 September that the alarm was raised about the sinking of the liner and several ships were sent out to search for survivors. When the ships returned on the afternoon of 2 October, the *Vesta* was in harbour and had survived the collision, despite the huge amount of damage. She had been alongside for two days by then and had already given accounts to the press but had assumed that the liner had survived the collision, never dreaming that the Arctic had gone down. No more survivors were found, despite several ships going out to search during the following week.

Although figures are ambiguous, it is thought that eighty-eight people survived the sinking of the *Arctic*, with anywhere between 285 and 372 victims. Three of those killed were the wife and two children of Collins Line founder Edward Collins. The problem with the lifeboats not being able to hold a full complement was brought up at the investigation, although this was again ignored. It would take the sinking of the *Titanic* for the shipping world to wake up and have that question raise its head again in a much larger way.

The sinking of the *Arctic* was a tragic prelude to what was to come many years later – a ship at speed in fog in collision (the *Andrea Doria* sinking, 1956) and having not enough lifeboats (as with the *Titanic*, 1912) along with a rescue operation that wasn't launched until it was realised that the ship had actually gone down. There were assumptions that held out along the way from the fact that it wasn't even realised that the ship was damaged to the tragedy of those left in the cold Atlantic after being tipped out of the lifeboats. The entire drama of this sea disaster is steeped in sadness and human nature's ability to panic when it comes to staring death in the face. Today, there is a memorial in a New York cemetery for a family of six who died on board the *Arctic*, but over 150 years on this shipwreck has been eclipsed so many times that people barely know it happened.

Her wreck has never been found.

Chapter 39

Pacific

Having a ship sink and the wreck not being found is understandable. It can only be found if somebody looks for it and, even then, the oceans are so large that people have spent lifetimes searching for shipwrecks with no luck. But what happens when a ship suddenly vanishes like the *Cyclops* or, in this case, the liner *Pacific*? How can hundreds of people and entire ships of this size suddenly vanish into thin air as if they never existed?

Owned by the Collins Line, the paddle-steamer *Pacific* was a sister ship to the *Atlantic*, *Baltic* and the sunken *Arctic* from the previous chapter. Built in New York, she was launched in 1849 to travel the same route as the *Arctic* with many hundreds of passengers over many voyages. At 2,707 gross tons, she was 281 feet long and could carry almost 300 passengers and 141 crew. It was the United States's goal to use these fast ships to win back trade in the passenger steamship business and take the dominance away from the UK. For this, the US Government subsidised the Collins' fleet in order to compete with the biggest rival Cunard, which was at the head of the game.

On 25 May 1850 the *Pacific* set sail on her maiden voyage to Liverpool with success and, later that year, won the Blue Riband trophy for fastest Atlantic crossing, from 11 to 21 September, keeping the prize for just under a year before her sister ship *Baltic* claimed it. Her voyages were pleasant enough for the passengers, not forgetting that such ships were new to the trade and people were just getting used to having the luxury of first-class travel at sea. But, on 4 December 1852, she was diverted to rescue the survivors from the barque *Jesse Stevens* in the mid Atlantic after she had gone down in a storm. The rescue was later immortalised in several paintings of the ship performing her humanitarian duty.

It was on 23 January 1856 that the *Pacific* set sail once again from Liverpool, a normal voyage that she had now achieved dozens of times and had become one of the fastest ships on the transatlantic route. She carried only forty-five passengers for this trip, a winter voyage always having fewer people on board, but still had her full complement of 141 crew led, by

Captain Asa Eldridge from Yarmouth, Massachusetts. He came from a seafaring family, the 46-year-old being the son of a ship's captain himself and a veteran of the sea from an early age who had also set a speed record two years before this voyage.

But the *Pacific* failed to arrive in New York when expected. As with any ship being overdue, especially in that day and age, a bit of leeway was given to allow for any delays, but nothing was heard of the ship. Ships departed their berths to head out and look for any signs of it, but there was no trace of anything – no wreckage, no bodies, nothing.

Considering that the *Arctic* disaster had strewn the sea with wreckage and dead people just two years before, the only conclusion that could be reached was that she had encountered an iceberg out at sea as she transited the areas off Newfoundland. In such freezing cold, it would be hard to survive in the lifeboats, let alone in the water. With no evidence to say otherwise, this was the only thing that could be said about the missing liner.

But this is where it gets stranger still, for a total of five years would pass until the lost ship would be mentioned again. A beachcomber in the Hebrides, a group of islands off the west coast of Scotland, came across a message in a bottle. This message read:

On board the *Pacific* from Liverpool to N.Y. - Ship going down. Confusion on board - icebergs around us on every side. I know I cannot escape. I write the cause of our loss that friends may not live in suspense. The finder will please get it published. W.M. GRAHAM.

Was this genuine? A check of the passenger list did find the name of a William Graham who was a British sea captain heading across the Atlantic as one of the few passengers on board. While it could possibly be a hoax, it is very random when considering that a lot of effort would have been given to this for it to seem genuine. The finder doesn't seem to have had their name go down in history as with other attention seekers in the past. For a bottle to have made it across the ocean is possible: there are cases such as that of a life-jacket from the *Lusitania* disaster in 1915 washing ashore in the Delaware River, Philadelphia, in 1920 and so it is entirely probable that this bottle was real.

For the Collins Line, the year the *Pacific* was lost was also the year that Congress cancelled their subsidy of the line. With both *Arctic* and *Pacific* gone that was 50 per cent of their ships left to continue their work. The company was now hitting financial difficulties with a decreasing reputation for reliability and struggling to survive. In just two years the Collins Line ceased to exist. The company had gone from providing the fastest ships in the world to nothing in just a few short years.

As for the ship herself, nothing was ever found of the *Pacific* at the time. Although a there was a report that a wreck found in the Irish Sea in 1991 was the missing liner, this was not substantiated and all evidence points to it not being the *Pacific*. The fact that there was nothing found at the time in such a small area, combined with the note in the bottle, would point to the ship being a lot further out to sea than anywhere near the British coastline.

But the loss of the *Pacific* and her 189 passengers and crew continues to be one of the most mysterious of all time, although there is very little written about it and, again, no major wreck expedition to attempt to solve it. Then again, with 4,000 miles of ocean to check between Liverpool and New York, who is to say where exactly she sank? Was it really an iceberg and, if so, how close to her destination did she get when it was encountered?

With more questions than answers, it will take a bit of luck to locate this wreck after over 150 years of silence and not even a rough idea of where she was last seen.

Chapter 40

Naronic

The *Pacific* was not the only passenger liner to vanish on a routine voyage. The same happened to the SS *Naronic*, a ship of the famous White Star Line in 1893. Built at the Harland and Wolff shipyard in Belfast, she was launched on 26 May 1892 and, in less than two months, was ready for her maiden voyage which commenced on 15 July, just four days after building work had been completed. She was 470 feet long and 6,594 gross tons. Her complement of fifty crew and around fifteen passengers made this cargo-carrying liner not only the world's largest but also a very quiet ship to be on.

Her main passengers though were those of the animal kind, for she was fitted out to carry livestock, over 1,000 at any one time, as well as general cargo. She was one of two sister ships, the *Bovic* doing the same run from Liverpool to New York and return but being put into service several weeks after her sister.

On 11 February 1893 the *Naronic* set sail on her seventh voyage from Liverpool to New York under the command of Captain William Roberts who had not long replaced her previous commanding officer. She had on board a total of fifty crew and twenty-four cattlemen tending to the cargo, the closest thing to passengers she would have on this trip.

Dropping the pilot off at Point Lynas, Wales, she headed out into open ocean and disappeared. The ship had never been out for longer than eleven days, so when day nineteen ticked by the *New York Times* felt the need to publicise this; her sister ship was much slower and even *Bovic* hadn't been out for this length of time before. She had departed on 17 February and had arrived at her destination already. This was now causing serious worry for the owners.

Nothing was seen or heard from the missing ship. Vessels coming in were questioned about the weather conditions, sea states and if they had seen the *Naronic*. All had been well, other than a bit of stormy weather slowing some ships down, but they had all made it. But, even at this point, on 1 March the White Star Line said that they had every reason to believe that she was safe and stressed just how well built the vessel was, highlighting the competency and skill of the crew who were making the voyage.

But, unbeknown to anybody on shore, the SS *Coventry* found a capsized lifeboat bearing the name of the missing liner floating in the sea in the early hours of 4 March. It was in good condition, its sail and mast attached as if it were being used as a sea anchor. Twelve hours later the ship found a second boat, although this one was swamped. The *Coventry* could not tell anybody about this until she, too, had reached port.

On 15 March, over a month after the *Naronic* had been last seen, the owners publicly declared their worry over the ship and held out hope that it was safe somewhere, although they said themselves that finding the ship would be unlikely. Rumours were all that the public had to go on and so stories of the ship carrying hundreds of immigrants were going around, which the White Star Line obviously denied.

On 19 March the *Coventry* was finally able to announce the discovery of the two boats over two weeks previously. By then it was obvious that the *Naronic* had gone down somewhere, but like the *Pacific* nobody knew when or where this had occurred, or for what reason. All they could do was mourn the loss of seventy-four people on an almost new ship.

All kinds of rumours were being thrown around to explain the loss, including sabotage. These were soon discounted. It turned out that the ship had not been insured and so the White Star Line had to take the loss completely, although the cargo on board was insured. The ship was soon replaced by others, but the mystery of what happened to *Naronic* wouldn't go away so easily.

In October 1893 the Norwegian ship *Emblem* claimed that they had found adrift a lifeboat from the wreck, upside down and covered in barnacles. From an examination of it, they seemed to believe that it had been hastily prepared which led them to think that the sinking was very sudden.

But then something even more mysterious happened. As with the lost *Pacific*, messages in a bottle started to appear, not one but a total of four.

The first was found off New York on 3 March 1893:

> *Naronic* sinking. All hand praying. God have mercy on us
> L Winsel
> 19th February 1893.

Bottle number two was found on 30 March at Ocean View, Virginia:

3:10 AM Feb.19. SS *Naronic* at sea. To who picks this up: report when you find this to our agents if not heard of before, that our ship is sinking fast beneath the waves. It's such a storm that we can never live in the small boats. One boat has already gone with her human cargo below. God let all of us live through this. We were struck by an iceberg in a blinding snowstorm and floated two hours. Now it 3:20 AM by my watch and the great ship is dead level with the sea. Report to the agents at Broadway, New York, M. Kersey & Company. Good bye all.
19th February 1893
John Olsen, Cattleman.

Number three was in the Irish Channel in June 1893:

Struck iceberg: sinking fast: *Naronic*
Young

The fourth and final bottle was in September 1893 in the river Mersey, UK:

All hands lost; *Naronic*; No time to say more … T

If we look at this at face value, we see a lot of evidence that the bottles were completely faked. First of all, the lifeboat found suggested that there had been a rush to get away, yet four different people had found time to have the same idea of writing a message in a bottle? Each message had been signed by someone different, yet none of the three names appeared on the manifest and 'T' could be anybody.

The iceberg theory was discounted also since no other ship had reported ice and the time of year was not one for vast numbers of icebergs, especially where the lifeboats were found. Considering that the lifeboats were drifting slowly and yet four bottles had separated and managed to get to opposite sides of the Atlantic in less time than it took for anything else makes all four bottles highly doubtful. A Board of Trade investigation discounted all of them as unreliable evidence and, most likely, a hoax.

With the wreckage taken into account, the *Naronic* is thought to have gone down mid-Atlantic in around the same area as *Titanic* would sink nineteen years later. What had caused the ship to sink is another matter, but it must have been so quick that no one could get to the boats in time to save themselves. Most likely the stormy weather may have played a part, but with very little to go on, the fate of the *Naronic* has always been a complete mystery.

Another sad part to this story is that there are no photographs of *Naronic* in existence. All stories have to use images of the sister ship *Bovic* or a drawing from the period. With so little information on this ship, she is very rarely written about and remains one of those tragic forgotten pieces of maritime history that are just begging to be revived and solved.

Chapter 41

Waratah

The loss of the liner *Waratah* was covered in my book *The 50 Greatest Shipwrecks*, but I cannot produce a book about missing ships without covering one of the most famous of them. She was a cargo and passenger liner built in Whiteinch, Scotland, and launched in 1908 for the Blue Anchor Line under the ownership of W. Lund and Sons. At 9,339 gross tons, *Waratah* was 465 feet long and could carry 432 passengers, with space for 600 more at a push, as well as 154 crew members.

She was built for the trade route between Australia and the UK to take a general cargo but also provide passengers with luxury accommodation for the long journey. She was also quite fast for a ship of her size and time; on her trials she reached a speed of 15 knots, which would make sure that the voyage was as short as possible. The extra few knots of speed could easily shave a large amount of time off a long-haul trip.

She sailed from London on her maiden voyage on 5 November 1908 with over 700 passengers and, by the 27th, was at Cape Town, arriving in Adelaide on 15 December, a total of forty days. During this time a small fire had ignited in one of the bunkers and continued re-igniting for several days. It was caused by the location of some of the steam valves heating up a non-insulated part of the deck head. Repairs were effected in Australia.

Captain Joshua Ilbery was concerned at this point about the ship's stability. He had previously commanded the *Geelong*, a sister ship on which *Waratah* was based on when she was built, and he had noticed a difference in the handling of the two ships. When the ship returned to Britain there were apparently some heated exchanges between the builders and owners regarding this problem but it seemed that nothing was to be done despite the misgivings of the captain. He wasn't happy with it and he raised the concern.

The liner made her second Australia trip on 27 April 1909 and took until 6 June to reach Adelaide, a journey that was fine, although heading on to Melbourne she ran into bad weather along the way.

By 25 July she had headed back north and arrived in Durban, South Africa, where one passenger, Claude Sawyer, sent a message to his wife in London stating that he was concerned about the ship. As a veteran of many sea journeys, and also an engineer, he stated that he thought the *Waratah* was unstable and left the ship to continue his journey to Cape Town by other means. To be that worried about a ship was quite something, even more so when he said that he had been disturbed by nightmares that he decided were a warning for him to get off the ship while he still could.

The following day at 2015 hours the *Waratah* departed Durban with 211 people on board heading to Cape Town for the next leg of the trip. She was spotted in the early hours of the morning on 27 July by the cargo ship *Clan Macintyre*. As the liner overtook, the ships exchanged messages by flashing light about their ships and destinations before heading on their way. By around 0930 the *Waratah* was over the horizon and gone ahead.

The 28th saw the cargo ship in a terrible storm as hurricane-force winds battered the *Clan Macintyre*. Further up the coast, several ships reported seeing a steamer including one vessel that later thought it looked as if explosions had occurred, but these were unconfirmed. Two soldiers on shore saw a ship that would later match the description of *Waratah* struggling in the heavy seas and then disappearing. They reported it to their camp but this was not taken seriously and the report was ignored.

The next day *Waratah* was due alongside Cape Town but, as the day wore on, it became evident that she was overdue. Some ships may take a while during a severe storm, so nobody was worried at that time. But when ships that had set off after *Waratah* started to make it to port the alarm bells were ringing.

It was 1 August when the first ship, a tug named *T.E. Fuller*, went out to conduct a search of the area, followed by several Royal Navy warships that were in the area. A false sighting led to an announcement that *Waratah* was afloat and heading to port slowly, but this was soon discounted, much to the disappointment of those still looking for her.

On the 13th the first bodies were found floating in the sea at *Waratah*'s last known position. Two ships reported seeing several corpses adrift in the sea and a tug was sent out to recover them but could not locate anything. If they had managed to recover any at the time this could at least confirm if they were from the missing ship.

After months of searching and several ships staying out at sea in the hope that she was adrift and looking for a tow, Lloyds of London officially posted the *Waratah* as missing on 15 December. But this did not stop the relatives of those missing from hiring a ship named *Wakefield* to carry on with the search. Needless to say, they came up with nothing.

From 1910 until 1939 there were several pieces of wreckage that may have come from the missing liner, including a life preserver with the ship's name, but many of these are unconfirmed reports or speculation.

The Board of Trade launched an inquiry in December 1910 in London and soon questions were being asked relating to the stability of the missing ship. Claude Sawyer was called to give his opinion, as were former passengers and crew from previous trips. Despite Lloyds giving it a good rating and saying that this ship was at the highest of standards regarding building and stability, the witnesses told a different story.

Stories of the ship rolling too far over in a storm, listing to one side and not re-righting herself fast enough, and the frequency of the ship listing even when the weather was good plagued the inquiry and the two sides to this story meant that no real conclusions could be reached regarding this. The sightings by several ships off the African coast could not all have been *Waratah* due to the huge distance between them in such a short space of time.

Many theories have come and gone regarding what happened to *Waratah*. Everything, from the cargo of concrete shifting in the storm causing her to roll over to a rogue wave, was considered although the ship that said it witnessed an explosion has not been discounted. With no evidence of any of this each theory is just as plausible as the next.

The loss of the *Waratah* has prompted an interest in this story over many years with one of those fascinated by it being Emlyn Brown. He began a serious search for the wreck in the early 1980s and, after painstaking research, conducted several expeditions into the 1990s until, finally, in 1999 a newspaper reported that his search had found a wreck that looked promising. But much to Brown's frustration, when a dive was conducted in 2001, the wreck the team had discovered was full of Second World War cargo. It was over thirty years too late to be the *Waratah*.

Research later concluded that this was the wreck of the cargo vessel *Nailsea Meadow*, torpedoed by a U-boat and sunk in 1943. Disappointed and with his research exhausted, Emlyn Brown abandoned the hunt for the *Waratah* wreck which today remains another undiscovered missing wreck.

Chapter 42

Californian

Of all the shipwreck stories in history, the sinking of the *Titanic* is the most famous, but one aspect of the *Titanic* story is how a nearby ship was said to have been able to go to the liner's aid but didn't. The incident has been a subject of debate for over 110 years and has led to books dedicated to just this one part of the story. This 'ship that stood still' during the sinking *Titanic* was the Leyland Line cargo/passenger liner *Californian*.

Built in Dundee and launched in 1901, the 447-foot-long ship was 6,223 gross tons and had room for forty-seven passengers and fifty-five crew. At the time she was actually the largest ship to be built in that city, highlighted by the fact that just taking the boilers through the streets to the shipyard actually damaged the road on which it was travelling.

Her aim was mainly to carry cargo and to offer passengers that were not in any rush to travel across the Atlantic a very basic accommodation for their journey, the ship making a top speed of 12 knots. On 27 March 1911 she had a new captain, Stanley Lord, a 33-year-old who had already been in charge of ships at sea for many years. By the start of 1912 *Californian* was fitted with a Marconi wireless set in a radio room with one operator, Cyril Evans, to man it twenty-four hours a day. This was not a problem. He would just work as much as possible until it was time for him to turn in for the night.

On 5 April 1912 *Californian* set sail from Liverpool heading across to Boston, Massachusetts with no passengers and the crossing was pretty much uneventful for the first nine days. On the evening of the 14th Evans was busy taking down ice reports that had been coming in all day from various ships in the area, transmitting others when they had seen them and that night the ship came upon even more ice that prompted the captain to stop. With so much ice around, Captain Lord decided they would stay where they were and proceed first thing in the morning. Evans radioed that to nearby ships but, due to the fact that the brand new luxury liner *Titanic* was very close by, the noise of the transmission caused the liner to respond

'Shut up, Shut up, I am busy, I am working Cape Race' before continuing with the regular radio traffic.

Feeling that was a little rude of them but, having done his job until late night, Evans switched his radio off and went to bed. On the bridge Third Officer Charles Groves and Second Officer Herbert Stone were watching a ship on the horizon and informed the captain. He suggested contacting her by Morse lamp but this heralded no response. The ship had also seemed to stop at around twenty minutes to midnight.

What did seem strange to them later in the night was that rockets were being fired from this mystery ship. The captain was informed this time by Second Officer Stone who asked if they were company signals. He said he did not know but to keep trying with the Morse lamp and let him know if anything changes.

As the night wore on, the rockets ceased and the ship had gone. What is shocking about this whole scenario is that, for the sake of a quick check, nobody woke the radio operator to see if there was anything amiss going over the airwaves.

What the *Californian* did not know was that the most infamous and tragic maritime disaster ever had just played out right under their noses. It was around 0400 hours when they caught sight of a steamer heading with all her lights on to the scene, the liner *Carpathia*. Lord woke up soon after and started to make plans to head out from the ice, telling the chief officer to wake Evans and find out what had been going on overnight. When he heard the news the crew of the *Californian* were shocked.

The largest liner in the world, the RMS *Titanic*, owned by the White Star Line, had been on her maiden voyage when at 2340 that night she had struck an iceberg that had opened up her hull below the waterline. She took less than three hours to sink and there were only enough lifeboats for half the 2,220 people on board, and not even that number managed to get off. *Carpathia* picked up a pathetic number of rickety boats and a total of 705 survivors. The exact death toll has always been open for debate, but a memorial to the sinking in Belfast has 1,512 names listed.

While *Carpathia* was hailed a hero upon her return to New York, the *Californian* was the subject of the anger that was now directed. How could a ship that was so clearly the closest to the disaster just stand there and do nothing? The subsequent British and American inquiries would pore over every minute of that night with a fine-toothed comb, but there was no denying that the crew of the *Californian* had made a fatal mistake that night.

Conflicting accounts of the night in question, along with the competency of the crew in dealing with such a situation, all became heavily scrutinised both in the courtrooms and the pages of the newspapers. *Titanic* survivors claimed that they had seen a ship in the distance but it was too far away to make out, never mind row to. Both inquiries blamed Captain Lord for failing to render assistance to the *Titanic*.

But in 1985, when the wreck of the *Titanic* was located, it was actually found thirteen miles away from her original reported position. *Californian* says she was nineteen-and-a-half miles away from *Titanic*, but the inquiries stated that it was much closer, but now this needed to be re-examined and, in 1992, a re-appraisal of evidence by the Marine Accident Investigation Branch concluded that, although the crew actions on board the *Californian* fell short of what was needed, the state of the ship trapped in ice would have not allowed it to get to the sinking until well after the disaster had taken place. Although this is still debatable over a century on, the evidence is clear to see and, in all truthfulness, the *Californian* was not going anywhere soon. Captain Lord was dismissed by the Leyland Line just months later but they did help him acquire a new role in a different company, his role in the sinking of the *Titanic* haunting him until his death in 1962.

For the *Californian*, her name would also always be associated with the *Titanic*. A year after being thrust into the spotlight, on 2 July 1913, she was damaged in a major fire in Veracruz, Mexico. At the outbreak of the First World War, she saw service as a transport for troops and cargo for the Allied campaign at Gallipoli, spending a lot of time in the warmer climates of the Mediterranean.

On 9 November 1915 she was off Greece, during a voyage from Salonica to Marseilles, when the ship was suddenly rocked by an explosion. She had been torpedoed by the German submarine *U-34* but, thankfully, was not completely finished yet. A French patrol vessel attached a tow line and started to pull her towards the safety of land, but a second U-boat had the *Californian* in her sights soon after. *U-35* fired at her and the resulting explosion this time killed one fireman and injured two others. The ship had no chance of being recovered now and she went down sixty miles south of Cape Matapan.

In the space of just three and a half years the *Californian* had made headlines through the *Titanic* disaster before being sunk herself during war service. But her legacy has lived on and whenever the subject of the *Titanic* comes up there is always talk of the *Californian*'s role in this not far away. Few people know that she sank during the war; to date the wreck has never been located despite a major interest in the *Carpathia* which suffered the same fate, which resulted in her wreck being located in 1999 and dived on.

It is hoped that, at some point soon, there will be enough renewed enthusiasm to warrant a search for this historic ship, bring back footage of the lost wreck and remember her for the ship she was, not the incident that made her infamous.

Chapter 43

Hans Hedtoft

A brand new passenger ship strikes an iceberg and sinks on her maiden voyage. Sounds familiar? Strange as it may seem, the *Titanic* was not the only ship to suffer this fate. This is the story of the Danish ship *Hans Hedtoft*.

Launched in Frederikshavn in Denmark on 13 August 1958, the name given to this new cargo and passenger vessel was taken from the former Danish politician and prime minister, Hans Hedtoft Hansen, who had died only three years before, a popular man who had been very critical of the Nazis after the invasion of his country. She was not a large ship, only 271 feet long and weighing in at 2,875 gross tons, her capacity being only 100 people at the most – sixty passengers and forty crew. Her main role was to provide a year-round service between Greenland and Denmark which means that she had to be built to withstand the conditions of this area.

Sporting a double bottom and an armoured bow and stern area, she was also armed with three anti-aircraft guns, 40mm weapons, provided by the Danish Ministry of Defence free of charge, although they were usually dismounted.

Her first voyage was a trip departing from Copenhagen on 7 January 1959 and she arrived in Greenland in record time, calling at four different ports before starting her return journey on the 29th with fifty-five passengers and forty crew. She had rather a special cargo on board, a large batch of archive material containing the history of Greenland – over 3 tons of material – and a Danish member of parliament Augo Lynge. Lynge was a busy man having time to write books, attend committees, edit a journal and father a total of nine children.

On the afternoon of 30 January, the US Coast Guard Cutter *Campbell* received a distress call from the *Hans Hedtoft* saying that the ship had struck an iceberg. Campbell responded to the call, as did a West German fishing vessel, *Johannes Kruss*, and another trawler nearby. Racing to the scene, another message was received stating that the ship was flooding in the engine-room. Her position was given as around 35 miles south of Cape Farewell, Greenland.

The last message ever heard from the *Hans Hedtoft* was received at 1741 hours which reported that the ship was sinking and requesting immediate assistance. A partial SOS received by the *Johannes Kruss* was cut off; after that the ships were met with complete silence.

The search and rescue operation was not at its peak. Aircraft in Newfoundland that could have assisted were grounded due to bad weather. The weather was not looking as if it was getting any better any time soon; if anything it was getting worse and slowing the ships that were trying to race to the scene.

On the 31st the *Campbell* found no trace of the missing ship and the conditions so bad that nothing could be achieved. The ships searched the area for over a week and found nothing. On 7 February the search was called off reluctantly. The entire ship and the ninety-five people on board had gone without trace.

Only on 7 October was a clue found – a lifebuoy washed ashore on the coast of Iceland.

The legacy of the loss of the *Hans Hedtoft* was the re-opening of an airfield in Greenland which had been closed only a few months before and a fund that was set up for the relatives of those killed. Today a memorial in Copenhagen pays tribute to the victims of the lost liner, unveiled by Queen Margrethe in 2005.

An ironic part to this story is that the rescue ship *Johannes Kruss* sailed from her home port of Bremerhaven on 21 February 1967 bound for the Atlantic fishing grounds. She was last seen 300 miles east of Cape Farewell and never seen again, all twenty-two crew on board presumed lost.

What is odd about this story is that very little wreckage was found and that the ship was fitted with a number of safety features such as five lifeboats, three of which could carry thirty-five people, two could carry twenty and four other inflatable rafts could hold further survivors with an automatic distress beacon fitted. The question people have pondered is why these boats were not launched? Why did the beacon not activate when she sank?

This ship was not the *Titanic*. She had navigational equipment and every possible reason to have, at least, some survivors. One theory was that her construction led to the sinking and Claude Enoch hoped to prove that in 2009 by searching for the wreck and bringing back the evidence to show the truth about whether his theory was correct or not. Whether he got enough sponsorship to mount the search is unknown but, at the time of writing, the wreck of the *Hans Hedtoft* remains as lost today as it was in 1959.

The mystery of the lost ship still opens up the debate about the dangers of icebergs. With the *Titanic* being the most famous ship to ever have struck ice, it is incredible that in the modern era there are still collisions. The Soviet cruise liner *Maxim Gorky* was holed in 1989 and almost 1,000 people had to be taken off the ship. Thankfully, the vessel was saved and was repaired. In 2007 the Antarctic cruise liner *Explorer* became another victim when she struck an iceberg off South Shetland Island in the Southern Ocean and all 154 people on board had to be rescued from boats drifting in the icy cold waters five hours later. Twenty hours after the collision, *Explorer* sank.

But still the mystery of what really happened to the Danish ship *Hans Hedtoft* rears its head now and again. Tragically, she is fast becoming a forgotten event, with so little information and very few people interested in resurrecting the story. We can only hope that one day there is a breakthrough in the hunt for the wreck.

Chapter 44

Lakonia

One of the worst things that can happen at sea is a fire, because when a ship burns there is no escaping the flames and smoke, unless you can evacuate straightaway. With any luck, a fire can be contained by cooling a compartment by spraying water on all six sides, but if that fire is allowed to spread then a ship can be in major trouble. Every year there are hundreds of fires on ships at sea, very few of them resulting in serious damage or the loss of a vessel, but for a cruise liner to burn and sink is the kind of incident that makes front-page headlines.

There were many liner fires throughout the last century, with names like *Paris*, *L'Atlantique*, *Normandie* and *Achille Lauro* which spring to mind. For some reason, the French lost several liners in the space of just a few years to fire, but in 1963 nobody could have dreamed that the thirty-three-year-old Greek liner *Lakonia* would have joined that list, especially as it was on a Christmas cruise with the height of the festivities being at the forefront of everyone's thoughts.

Lakonia started life as the Dutch *Johan van Oldenbarnevelt* when she was launched on 3 August 1929. Her service to the Netherland Line made her a favourite amongst travellers to the Dutch East Indies; at 586 feet long, she was over 19,000 gross tons and could accommodate almost 800 passengers with 360 crew members, as well as having the capacity to carry around 9,000 tons of cargo in her holds.

Her engines could push a good 19 knots cruising speed and this served her well during the Second World War when Holland-America Line chartered her to be used as a cargo ship between the Caribbean and New York. As Holland fell to the Nazis, *Johan van Oldenbarnevelt* was requisitioned as a troopship for the Allies and was managed by the Orient Line to carry up to 4,000 troops on voyages that took her around the world all the way to the Far East until she was finally returned to her owners in 1946. Over time, she was used again for troop transport during the Indonesian independence fighting and then returned to cruising where she carried on as before, making her last trip around the world in 1962.

She was sold on 8 March 1963 to the Shipping Investment Corporation, a Greek company that renamed her *Lakonia* and carried out a vast amount of renovation on the ship. With extra cabins, air conditioning, various new features and an increase to over 20,000 gross tons, she was ready to cruise from Southampton under the operators Ormos Shipping Company, also known as the Greek Line.

Making her first voyage on 24 April 1963, *Lakonia* was performing well and the passengers loved her, with over two dozen cruises already planned for the following year following a mini-refit in early December 1963.

A few days after work was completed, *Lakonia* set sail from Southampton under the command of Captain Mathios Zarbis on 19th December for what was planned to be a Christmas cruise lasting eleven days around the Canary Islands, starting with Madeira. On board were 1,022 people – 646 passengers and 376 crew – most of the passengers being British, while most of the crew were either German or Greek.

Twenty-four hours earlier the ship had passed a safety inspection and had all the certificates needed to sail. Not only that, but she had had a new fire-alarm system installed, new equipment and twenty-four lifeboats. A boat drill was carried out on the 20th as the ship was at sea heading south, but many passengers didn't bother turning up.

It was 2300 hours on the 22nd that a steward was walking past the ship's hairdressers and noticed what looked like smoke coming from the gap under the door. When he went to investigate, he saw that the entire shop was on fire and, within seconds, it was spreading out into the corridor. Another steward nearby saw the drama and tried to help by attempting to fight the fire with extinguishers, but it already seemed to be out of control. One of them ran off to raise the alarm but, when the alarms sounded, they seemed very quiet and most passengers didn't hear a thing.

Lakonia was 180 miles north of the island of Madeira. Thankfully, many passengers were still up and about in the ballroom, but the smoke was spreading fast, although many dismissed it as tobacco from cigars and thought no more about it. By then the public address system was out of action, the damage being quick and so no word could get out. However, many were starting to realise that something was not right and, at around 2330, the smoke had well and truly entered the ballroom where passengers were being herded onto the upper decks.

Orders and information were coming in thick and fast, but the instructions were confusing for passengers who were told to go one way, but that was in the path of the fire, while some people were trapped in cabins and found themselves cut off. At around the same time, the first distress calls were sent asking for assistance from any ships in the area. The upper deck was feeling the heat as the fire reached the radio room and no more transmissions could be made. The ship was in a very bad state and at 0100 the order was given to abandon ship via the lifeboats.

Scared passengers in nightclothes and evening attire filled the boats, but some boats had already been destroyed in the flames. Others, badly in need of maintenance, had rusted on the davits and couldn't be shifted.

Some crew members were seen to leave before the passengers, which sparked anger since the boats were getting away and leaving onboard people who didn't know what they were doing. Some jumped overboard and died instantly, striking the ship on the way down. In the meantime, explosions rocked the ship.

The first rescue ship, *Salta*, an Argentine passenger vessel, arrived on the scene at 0330 hours followed by the British merchant ship *Montcalm* half an hour later. More ships raced to the scene and aircraft flew overhead dropping survival aids and life rafts to those in the water. The last person to leave *Lakonia* alive was the captain.

Survivors were hurried to Madeira, a few others went east to Morocco, but a total of 128 people had been killed in the disaster, ninety-five of whom were passengers. Many had died as a result of the evacuation and being injured going overboard.

As the days went by the flames died down. The aircraft carrier HMS *Centaur* sent a boarding team over on Christmas Eve to recover the bodies of those who had been killed. The blackened derelict looked as if the ship was caving in on itself. The Norwegian tug *Herkules* attached a line and attempted to tow the ship to Gibraltar although it was listing, and with holes all over the superstructure and decks.

Slowly the *Lakonia* was taken eastwards for the next few days, but the struggle to keep the ship afloat was a losing battle as the list increased until the afternoon of the 29th when she sank stern first, 230 miles south-west of Lisbon, Portugal. Several members of the crew, including the captain, were charged with negligence; the cause of the fire was said to be faulty wiring.

To date, her wreck has never been found but, judging by the state of her hull at the time of the boarding party going onboard, she is most likely in a collapsed mess on the seabed with very little standing tall. A sad end to a ship so loved by those she had hosted in her years at sea.

Chapter 45
Lyubov Orlova

The tabloid press loves a good story, the more ridiculous the better, so when the speculation about the fate of the liner *Lyubov Orlova* was reported they had a field day with the headlines. Built in Yugoslavia and designed with an ice-strengthened hull for cruises around the Antarctic and Arctic regions, she was named after a Russian singer and actress. She was operated from the Russian port of Vladivostok during the Soviet Union era.

Launched on 3 November 1975, she was 295 feet long and 4,251 gross tons, with a carrying capacity of 110 passengers and seventy crew. Compared to most liners, this was a relatively small ship, catering for the unique experience that would allow tourists to view the ice from a safe distance and had several refurbishments during her lifetime as the USSR collapsed and gave way to her being Russian owned and operated.

In 2006 she ran aground at Deception Island in Antarctica and had to be towed off. Four years later the operators, Cruise North Expeditions, had accumulated a mountain of debt relating to, among other things, the crew not being paid. Inspectors boarding the ship on 2 July 2010 were shocked by the condition of the vessel. A huge amount of safety equipment was defective and the crew's procedures were well below standard. The inspecting officer was then bribed by the captain, a report on which went straight to the police.

The *Lyubov Orlova* was seized in St John's, Newfoundland but, instead of all the problems being sorted, the liner was left where it was and stayed there abandoned by her owners and crew.

The ship stayed alongside St John's for over two years. People who had served on her or travelled as a passenger were shocked to learn the state in which she had been left. She was never on the scale of a luxurious ship by any stretch of the imagination, but she was presentable and serviceable and could do her job without any problems. Now the ship had accumulated a debt totalling over $2 million in unpaid wages, costs and port fees which the owners were simply not going to pay.

She listed in harbour over time, the port authorities concerned that she would sink while alongside, so more money was spent just trying to keep her afloat. What made it worse was the fact that it wasn't just the ship that was left to its own devices; over fifty crew members still lived on board. Their visas would only extend to working on board the ship and so they couldn't just get other jobs nearby. Eventually, they had to be fed by charity parcels donated by the Red Cross and Salvation Army as well as sympathetic locals.

As the supplies ran out, the crew were sent home on flights and the *Lyubov Orlova* was finally left alone and derelict, slowly deteriorating as the defects caused by the vessel's lack of maintenance gradually worsened. As water spread around the ship from burst pipes, the smell became horrendous and attracted vermin. A company bought the ship but they, too, struggled with the debt that it seemed to accumulate.

Eventually, the only thing that could be done to the liner was to scrap it, so on 23 January 2013 a tug named *Charlene Hunt* connected up her lines and pulled her away from what had become her home. After so long tied up, she began the slow journey from her berth in St John's to the Caribbean Island of the Dominican Republic. The sad state of the once-grand ship was noticed by few as the vessel slowly made her way out to sea and away from land for her final journey.

Incredibly, the story of the *Lyubov Orlova* then became headlines. For once the ship made the news, but long after her career had taken a nosedive. Just a day after leaving St John's the towline had parted, leaving the derelict liner adrift in the Atlantic. The tug couldn't get a line back on board and it would be over a week before another ship attempted a tow, but again the line parted as the ships struggled in heavy seas.

On 31 January the offshore supply vessel *Atlantic Hawk* managed to get a line on board and pulled her out of the way of the oil platforms in the area. The thought of this ship colliding with an oil- or gas-rig didn't bear thinking about and it was in everyone's interest to get the ship as far away from danger as possible. As soon as the danger had passed, the *Lyubov Orlova* was simply cut loose and allowed to drift out to sea.

But by then the ship was in international waters. The cost of saving it outweighed what it would owe when it came to letting it sink, so it was abandoned in mid-ocean after it was deemed to be not carrying pollutants. It did, however, carry EPIRB (Emergency Position Indicator Radio Beacons), as fitted to all ships, that generated a signal when immersed in water and designed to float free if a ship went down. The two held onboard activated but on different days – 23 February and 12 March 2013, although a ship had in fact sighted her afloat on 23 February when she was only 1,300 nautical miles from the coast of Ireland.

A search of the area found a sole lifeboat from the ship, the only evidence that the *Lyubov Orlova* had ever been in that area. By then it was assumed that the ship had sunk and that was the end of that story.

But the following year the liner was in the news again as several tabloid newspapers ran a story that suggested that it was actually still afloat and the fact that, since over a year had passed since she left port, the rats that had been breeding on board had nothing to eat and were feasting on each other. Headlines talking of a 'cannibal-rat infested ghost ship' made fascinating and highly amusing reading but, of course, this didn't happen. The story that the ship had stayed afloat, and had become home to a horror story, was pure speculation.

When that part of the story died down, another reported that a wreck had been found ashore in California and could be the missing liner. Images of the ship buried in sand showed a vessel that, clearly, had been there for many years, heavily flattened over time and clearly not the missing liner. She was in fact the SS *Monte Carlo* which had grounded in a storm on Coronado Island, California in 1937. Strangely the newspapers never speculated on how a liner could drift from being close to Ireland all the way around to the other side of the world and then bury itself on a beach on the American west coast. Once again, the story of the *Lyubov Orlova* made the news, but for the most ridiculous of reasons.

So, a ship that had few headlines in her life ended up making the news long after she had gone down, her wreck somewhere mid-Atlantic over a thousand miles from land. But the false reports kept the story of the ship alive and allowed people to check out the history of this vessel, bringing up happier memories amongst veterans of the old cruises in which she had originally partaken. But, despite her sad state at the end, she will now always be known as the 'Ghost Ship of Cannibal Rats' which then became the title of a song on the Canadian rock band Billy Talent's 2016 album *Afraid of Heights*.

Never has there been a stranger legacy for a ship that did nothing in the final years of her life.

Part VI
Aircraft

Chapter 46

Italia and the death of Amundsen

So now this book turns onto the mysterious disappearances that have happened at sea involving aircraft. As with many aeroplane crashes, those that are out at sea are the most difficult ones to attain the cause, primarily because the wreckage drifts for long periods before it is located, making it harder to determine where the main body and the heavy remnants lie.

But for this we can start with not an aeroplane, but an airship. Designated N-4, the *Italia* was built by the Italian Air Force in the mid-1920s, making her first flight on 15 April 1928 for her operators, the Italian Geographical Society. This huge semi-rigid airship was 347.8 feet long with a gas capacity of over 650,000 cubic feet, her three engines powering her across the sky at over 70 miles per hour.

Designed by General Umberto Nobile, funding was found for this huge aircraft to be used in scientific exploration at the North Pole with assistance from the military, an expedition that would hopefully generate a lot of publicity and success along the way. So, on her first-ever flight the airship took to the skies from Milan and headed to the Arctic with twenty people on board, stopping in Germany thirty hours later to check on damage caused by hailstones. Repairs took over a week and, eventually, the *Italia* set off, heading north on 3 May 1928, taking just eight hours to reach Stockholm, mooring early the following morning in Finland during a blizzard.

The next day it flew, again back on course, and arrived in Kings Bay on 6 May, three weeks after it had departed her home country. She was now in the Arctic and several journeys across the ice commenced over the coming days. It was on the journey back from her third trip that the Italia struggled with the wind. With sixteen crew on board, the journey back to Kings Bay was fast turning into a nightmare.

Battling a strong wind was using too much fuel, the altitude was dropping and the crew struggled to gain any speed but, on the morning of 25 May, *Italia* crashed tail-first into the ice, the control cabin smashing down seconds later. Detaching from the rest of the craft, the weightless air bag rose back up and drifted away. What was left on the ice were one dead, nine survivors and six left clinging to the airship still. The position was seventy-five miles north of Svalbard, with little hope of rescue any time soon. The ice that they were on was drifting slowly and their position was changing all the time. All they could do was wait and hope.

In the days that followed, the survivors had little to do but try and stay alive. The wreckage of the gondola contained food and navigational instruments and a tent to shelter, so they had the barest minimum for the time being. But many were not dressed to be exposed to Arctic weather conditions.

Unbeknown to them, a rescue operation was already under way and the polar teams were already chartering boats to head out to search for the lost airship. One of those who volunteered to search was famed Norwegian explorer Roald Amundsen. He had made a name for himself by being the first person to reach the South Pole in 1911 and then the first to reach the North Pole in 1926.

News spread fast that the *Italia* was missing and every explorer in the area raced to the scene to volunteer. The only problem was there was no organisational aspect and it all seemed so very slapdash.

Meanwhile, the survivors managed to get a radio and transmit distress messages, one partial message being picked up by a ship, but it was not passed on. The weather prevented any other messages getting through to the rescue parties but an amateur radio operator in a Russian village did something, but could not be sure of the location.

By 18 June the airship had been missing for twenty-four days with no sign of the aircraft or the crew. Amundsen was still very much involved in the rescue operation and he was in a Latham 47 flying-boat with two pilots and three Frenchmen, scouring the icy wasteland for any sign of the wrecked *Italia*. Heading to Spitsbergen, the aircraft continued the never-ending viewing of the land around the island of North East Land.

On board the aircraft were enough supplies to enable a rescue operation to take place on the ice, should they locate the missing sixty people. Parachutes were attached to food and equipment so that they could be dropped easily and the exact position reported back. But Amundsen and his crew never reported the location of the survivors, for the aircraft never returned to base.

Two more days would pass. By then there was a search on for *Italia* and the flying-boat. Incredibly, the *Italia* survivors were found on 20 June and supplies were dropped by an Italian pilot, although most were destroyed on impact. Three days passed and another aircraft managed to rescue one survivor but crashed in the return attempt to rescue the rest, the two occupants not being rescued for almost two more weeks on the ice.

Incredibly, two *Italia* survivors were found trekking across the ice on 11 July and rescued by an icebreaker the day after, along with five others. Another aircraft had been lost but the five crew members were picked up the same day as the *Italia* seven.

With a total of eight survivors, the focus turned to figuring out what went wrong. The survivors told the story of the struggle to keep the *Italia* from being battered by the wind and the eventual crash into the Arctic ice. In the meantime, wreckage was found off the coast of Tromsø, Norway. This was identified as coming from the aircraft flown with Roald Amundsen and his team. A wing float and a fuel tank were all that was left of one of the greatest polar explorers in history.

It is incredible to think that the survivors of the *Italia* managed to survive the best part of two months on the ice. Other than the six who vanished with the airship, the remaining bunch only lost two of their team; one died during the trek for help while another died in the crash itself. However, the *Italia* was never located.

There have been attempts to find the wreckage. The latest in 2018 had a seabed search for any remains come up with nothing. By 2009 there had already been several hunts for the wreckage of Amundsen's plane, again with no luck.

As it stands, both aircraft are still officially missing, their wreckage in such a large area that it may be many years yet before an explorer gets lucky.

The legacy of Roald Amundsen lives on, his exploits the focus of a museum where two of his ships, the *Fram* and *Gjoa*, are preserved in Oslo. There people can learn about this remarkable man who died trying to save his fellow explorers from the bitter realms of the Arctic ice.

Chapter 47

Amelia Earhart

Since the Wright brothers' first manned flight in a flimsy aircraft in 1903, the world of aviation has come such a long way in a relatively very short space of time. One of the people who pioneered long distance flying was Amelia Earhart, a girl from Kansas who would go up in an aircraft for the first time just seventeen years after it had been made possible. This sparked an obsession that made Earhart a name that would live on in history.

After the first time she stepped onboard an aircraft she loved it. Within a year she had not only booked on flying lessons but she had bought her first plane, becoming qualified to fly after two years' training. When a female was sought to fly across the Atlantic Ocean, she was head-hunted to be the one to do it. On 18 June 1928 she completed the flight after taking off from Newfoundland the day before, instantly becoming a celebrity across the world. This started her career off where she lectured about her adventure, writing a book titled *20 Hrs, 40 Min* which was published the same year. SS

Not content with just one headline-hitting flight, she did it again from Newfoundland to Londonderry in Northern Ireland on 20-21 May 1932 where she smashed the record in just four minutes under fifteen hours. She had to divert from her planned destination of Paris due to problems with her aircraft but she had still achieved a remarkable feat. After this, she carried out a number of inter-state flying and promoting women to follow her lead in doing things that were out of the ordinary. She became a role model for women across the world and actively encouraged potential female pilots to push for their goals.

Another solo flight from Hawaii to California made her a record breaker once again, doing it in seventeen hours and seven minutes in 1935. That year she flew another solo from Los Angeles to Mexico. It seemed that there was nothing she couldn't do, nowhere she couldn't fly. So, she started planning for the ultimate challenge, one that had never been done before – to fly around the world with just a navigator.

The aircraft that she was going to use was a twin-engine Lockheed Electra, officially starting in Miami on 1 June 1937 and heading out over the Atlantic Ocean. She had already hopped across the States over the previous week; this time she would hop across to the Caribbean island of Puerto Rico. Each day would be a new destination where she and her navigator, Fred Noonan, would rest and prepare for the next part of the trip. It was not going to be easy: sitting in the pilot's seat when aircraft had only been invented just thirty years before was a huge pioneering task and each milestone was celebrated as they came closer to the next stop and the final destination.

Over the next four weeks the aircraft touched down in Venezuela, Surinam, Brazil, Senegal, the Anglo-Egyptian Sudan, India, Burma, Siam, the Dutch East Indies, Australia and, finally, Lae in New Guinea where they stopped for several days. By then they had done 22,000 miles with the 7,000 that remained mostly over the Pacific Ocean where there were only two stops, Howland Island and Hawaii, before they would reach Oakland, California, their final landing stop. They took off from Lae in the morning of 2 July and headed out towards Howland Island which would take them around twenty hours. Each step of the way, Earhart would keep in touch by radio and report position, altitude and any other details. By 1500 hours that afternoon she reported 10,000 feet altitude, with thick clouds later causing her to reduce to 7,000, and that her speed was 150 knots. Due to the International Date Line and the time zones being used, the date was still 2 July with the time technically earlier than when they set off.

Meanwhile the US Coast Guard Cutter *Itasca* was off the destination island to offer help such as ferrying news reports to the island and providing navigation/communications assistance if required. It could also guide the aircraft towards the island using a homing signal if they so needed. There was a slight bit of confusion with this, however, with Earhart scheduling her communications in GMT and the ship using a naval time zone system. In addition, the signals between aircraft and ship were not fully synchronised. The aircraft transmitted at 0758 hours, saying that they could not hear the ship and asked for transmissions on voice so that the direction finding could locate the position. This was unsuccessful.

The island was hard to locate at the best of times but, according to the transmissions heard from the aircraft, they believed they were at the required position. However, the ship could see no aircraft. *Itasca* fired up her boilers to generate smoke so that the aircraft would be able to see something, but again nothing was seen.

Some garbled messages were heard but these were indistinguishable. Her scheduled radio call at 0815 hours did not happen. Weak signals were said to be heard but some have been dismissed as hoaxes. The aircraft was somewhere close to the island, but how close nobody seemed to know.

By then it was clear that the aircraft was missing since fuel would have run out. Ships in the area started a huge operation to try to find the aircraft on the assumption that it had ditched at sea. Using only the scant information of their last few hours of radio transmissions, the search scoured the Pacific for the lost Electra. By 19 July the search was called off with no sign of the plane.

The disappearance of Amelia Earhart has been seen as one of the greatest aviation mysteries ever. Just where did she fly off to? Where did the plane end up? Whatever the truth, she was legally declared dead on 5 January 1939 so that her husband could manage her estate and finances.

Conspiracies have been rife with the loss of the two flyers, one of them being that they survived a crash and were captured by the Japanese and executed, highly unlikely and one for which there is no evidence.

A group known as The International Group for Historic Aircraft Recovery, also known as TIGHAR, has been researching this incident for over thirty years with some fascinating discoveries and some serious research coming to light. A credible theory that the aircraft had crashed on the island of Nikumaroro, also known as Gardner Island, was given credence when a photograph emerged of a shipwreck from 1929. The SS *Norwich City* had gone aground on the reef and was still there when Earhart's plane vanished. In this photograph of the wreck taken many years later, an image of an aircraft wheel sticks up out of the water. With other evidence pointing towards this area, ocean explorer Robert Ballard launched an expedition in 2019 to search the whole area for evidence of the lost Electra. There was nothing there, but Ballard has vowed to return to complete the search at a later date.

With so many theories about what happened to this lost aircraft, nobody is any closer to knowing the truth. In the meantime, Amelia Earhart has gone down in history as a great pioneering aviator with her life ending in one of the most mysterious aircraft disappearances of all time. More conspiracies come to light every year, including one that showed a photograph of two people who looked like the missing flyers from a distance under capture by the Japanese. It later came to light that the photo was from a Japanese travel guide published two years before the plane went missing.

Amelia Earhart's legend lives on in books, films, documentaries and monuments. Where she remains today is another question, but one that will not go away until she is found.

Chapter 48
Amy Johnson

While Amelia Earhart was making headlines from America, Amy Johnson was taking the crowns for Britain in the aviation world. Born in Hull, East Yorkshire, on 1 July 1903, she had a keen interest in flying from an early age and got her pilot's licence in 1929, later becoming the first woman to get a ground engineer's C licence on top of that. She raised funds via her father in order to purchase her first aircraft, a de Havilland DH.60 Gipsy Moth which she named *Jason* and flew solo from Croydon in Surrey to Darwin, Australia. That journey was an incredible piece of aviation endurance for the time and she became the first woman to fly solo from England to Australia.

Immediately, she became a celebrity and people started to recognise the name Amy Johnson, the girl from Hull who was now giving Amelia a run for her money. She was appointed CBE in the 1930 King's Birthday Honours list as well as receiving a number of other awards, but this didn't mean her flying career was done. In fact, she didn't just want to stop there. With her aircraft now ready to be displayed in a museum, she purchased one she named *Jason II*, another aircraft of similar build, a de Havilland DH.80 Puss Moth, which she then flew from London to Moscow, together with a co-pilot, in one day, landing and refuelling before continuing even further soon after, heading to Tokyo in Japan and once again setting a record time.

On she went with a London to Cape Town trip which, by 1933, ended up with her doing a trans-Atlantic trip in a de Havilland DH.84 Dragon named *Seafarer*, from Wales to New York, with her new husband, Jim Mollison, as the co-pilot. She got as far as Connecticut before having to crash land where she and Jim suffered minor injuries. But this didn't stop her wanting to keep flying, and the Americans loved what she had done. When they recovered the two of them were shown off in a ticker-tape parade down Wall Street. In 1934 they went to India during a race from Britain to Australia, although they had to pull out there due to engine problems.

Another record breaker was Britain to South Africa in 1936, the year she divorced Jim and reverted to her maiden name of Johnson. At that time, she was quite a celebrity and even had a fashion brand. By the start of the Second World War, she was flying for the Portsmouth, Southsea and Isle of Wight Aviation Company, doing trips over the Solent and providing practice for the searchlight teams training for when German bombers started coming over.

With the company being taken over by the Air Ministry in March 1940 she was made redundant and so she joined the Air Transport Auxiliary (ATA) which had the role of ferrying military aircraft around the country for the RAF. She held the rank of First Officer and seemed to enjoy her job, writing an article for the *Woman Engineer* journal which was published after her death.

On 5 January 1941 Amy Johnson boarded an Airspeed Oxford, a twin-engine monoplane, for a journey from Prestwick, stopping at RAF Squires Gate in Blackpool, and landing at her final destination at RAF Kidlington near Oxford. But she never landed at Oxford. Instead, she found herself in bad weather over the Thames Estuary near Herne Bay.

Struggling to find her way and out of fuel, she was forced to bale as her aircraft crashed into the river not far from Knock John Buoy on Tizard Bank. Her parachute was seen by a group of passing ships that raced to the scene to effect a rescue, but the heavy seas and rough weather made this almost impossible. The balloon-barrage ship HMS *Haslemere* was close to her as she struggled in the water and shouted for help. The crew threw ropes for her to grab on to, but she was already suffering from the intense cold of the freezing water and getting weaker by the second. Still wearing her helmet, some members of the crew would swear they saw two bodies in the water at that point, although nobody is sure where this came from.

Unable to grab hold of the ropes, Amy was seen to go under the ship. The captain, Lieutenant Commander Walter Fletcher dived into the sea to try to save her and a lifeboat was launched to bring them both back in. But, tragically, he died a few days later in hospital.

The only thing recovered from the aircraft was her watertight flying bag, a chequebook and her log book, which were found washed up nearby. Her body was never found.

Several people came forward giving different views of this incident, one claiming he shot her down after twice giving the wrong identification code. Another said that she was killed by the ship's propellers, but this was a second-hand story.

Since her death, Amy Johnson has been commemorated in many ways. Although she has no known grave, she is on a number of memorials, including the Air Force Memorial at Runnymede, a statue in her home city of Hull and a variety of plaques around the country, not to mention the number of actual buildings named in her honour.

Amy's parents donated some of her possessions to Sewerby Hall, a former stately home and now a museum near the East Yorkshire town of Bridlington where they remain on display to this day. There has been talk over the years of a search for Amy's plane, the crash site still not located, although no sign of Amy's aircraft was ever found.

Her legacy resembles that of Amelia Earhart. Both women were very much alike in that they were inspirational, pioneering women flyers who broke records, both solo and with co-pilots/navigators. Their deaths mirrored each other with the mystery just four years apart, one vanishing on a world tour, the other in the service of her country. Neither have any grave but the sea.

Chapter 49

L-8

The loss of the airship *Italia* is a unique disaster as there have been very few mysterious incidents involving those behemoths of the sky. Most of the major events, such as the crash of the *Hindenburg* and *R-101* in the 1930s, were headline hitting and shocking, but they also heralded the death of passenger travel by airship. However, the airship was not gone for good. The US Navy used this enormous piece of equipment for its own use as a capable reconnaissance tool that could drift silently over enemy territory without so much as a sound while the occupants took photographs or, as with the Germany's Zeppelins during the First World War, drop bombs on towns below.

The Goodyear Aircraft Company built a number of training airships known as blimps in the 1930s and the US Navy awarded a contract for two types of these advertising aircraft to be used for their facilities, these would be K-Class and L-Class and each one would be designated accordingly with a number. Their main role would be coastal patrols, the L-Class would be 147.5 feet long with a gas volume of 123,000 cubic feet, her two engines giving a maximum speed of 61 miles per hour.

L-8 was one of the aircraft used for these patrols and although they would never be put in a combat role, these blimps were useful for training serials and patrols that involved submarine hunting after the war started for America at the end of 1941.

By April 1942 the *L-8* was tasked to deliver vital aircraft parts to the aircraft carrier USS *Hornet* that was about to carry out the famous Doolittle Raid on Japan to demonstrate that America could hit them just as much as they had struck at Pearl Harbor.

It was a normal submarine patrol that had *L-8* take off from Treasure Island in San Francisco at 0603 on the early morning of 16 August 1942. As part of Airship Patrol Squadron 32, the two men assigned to the airship that day were 27-year-old pilot Lieutenant Ernest DeWitt Cody who would be assisted by his co-pilot, 35-year-old Ensign Charles Adams, making his first flight as a commissioned officer, although he had already been in the Navy for fifteen years.

On board was one machine gun of 0.30 calibre along with two depth charges should they spot a submarine and need to drop them. The blimp had only been inspected recently and was found to be in good condition, this being its 1,092nd trip.

As the *L-8* slowly and silently made its way around the coast there was something amiss down below, just four miles off the Farallon Islands. An oil slick was seen on the surface and the crew radioed back to Treasure Island at 0738 hours. On the ocean a nearby fishing vessel and a Liberty ship saw the airship drift down for a closer look and circle the area of the oil slick.

Just over an hour later at 0850 hours the controllers at Treasure Island lost contact with the blimp and, minutes later, just after 0900, the aircraft was seen to drop ballast and ascend back to its regular height and head east, although little did they know that it was almost opposite to its intended course. Normally, an update would follow something like this but *L-8* did not transmit anything, neither did they send off their position at 0800 hours, nor did a scheduled report at 0930 arrive. The control room was not too worried and thought it may have been a radio malfunction; the crew were competent and the weather was good, but a sighting from an aircraft was starting to cause concern when they reported seeing a blimp out of control nearby.

On the western coast of San Francisco is Ocean Beach, an area just off Golden Gate Park, and it was there at 1115 hours that morning that observers noticed something peculiar. Heading towards them at very low altitude was *L-8* which seemed to be drifting without a particular heading. The lines were dangling down and two fishermen grabbed hold of them and tried to steady the craft; but it was far too heavy and out of control for them to do anything, but they did see one thing that was strange – the gondola door was open and the cab itself was not occupied.

The fishermen being forced to let go eventually, the blimp rose again and ran into a nearby hill which dislodged one of the depth charges which gave it enough weight loss to ascend further but an automatic valve started releasing helium gas which caused the bag to deflate slowly. Taking a journey out of control over a golf course and down Mission Street, a crowd of curious people were following the huge aircraft as it drifted over the houses of the neighbourhoods. As the airship became less able to keep in the air the *L-8* clipped the roofs of homes and telegraph poles before finally crashing into the front of a house, number 419 Bellevue Avenue, Daly City, just south of San Francisco itself. The aircraft had drifted over the land for around fifteen minutes after it had come onto the beach.

The military and local police gathered at the crash site. Everybody who saw it was confused by the fact that the two crew members were not only missing but they had not been occupying the gondola since it was first sighted coming in from the Pacific. A search and rescue operation was launched immediately up and down the coast in the hope that Cody and Adams would be found alive but, with all the survival equipment found still onboard the blimp and the equipment in full working order, it seemed that *L-8* had not been in distress and the crew had not been forced to evacuate the aircraft through an onboard emergency. Whatever had happened, it must have happened too quickly to be able to send a distress call.

An investigation was launched by the US Navy to determine the circumstances of the loss of the two men. The evidence of the eyewitnesses who saw the blimp head towards the oil slick suggested that the only plausible theory was that they had perhaps descended to drop a smoke marker and as they opened the door one of them fell out and the other tried to recover him but fell with him. This would have caused a sudden weight loss for the blimp which would explain it rising again suddenly and heading in the wrong direction. As this is just a theory, although as good an explanation as could be figured out, the truth about this matter is still just as much a mystery today as it was back in 1942.

L-8 was repaired and found herself back in service not long after the crash, eventually being sold back to Goodyear and renamed *America*, flying over sporting events until 1982 when it was eventually retired. Today the gondola is painted in its original colours as *L-8* and is on display in the National Naval Aviation Museum in Pensacola, Florida.

Two missing airmen were declared legally dead in 1943.

Chapter 50

Leslie Howard

In this day and age you could name a dozen famous people who have
died in a plane crash. When their names appear in the media, fans are
shocked but, to the investigators, it's just another air disaster. With
people like Buddy Holly, Kobe Bryant and the Manchester United football
team becoming victims of aviation's most tragic days, it would be beneficial
to take the reader back to when one of the first such stars appeared on
that list.

Born Leslie Howard Steiner, he had dropped the German sounding
surname by 1920 as his acting career had started to take off when he made
the transition from bank clerk to Army officer and finally to theatre star.

Born in London in 1893, Howard soon became well known in the
showbiz world and started his own film company with several others at
much the same time as he changed his name.

It didn't take long before he was making and starring in big screen films
that were shown around the world, his name soon becoming that of a
major actor when his greatest effort was his role as the lead character in
Gone with the Wind (1939). With the outbreak of the Second World War
his acting career took a different turn. This time he turned his attention to
making war films that would inspire the public and feed their imagination.
He had come back from America to help his country in the war effort and
if he couldn't fight himself he could certainly provide those back home
with entertainment.

Howard made every effort to promote the British wherever he went,
especially in the dark days of the war. In May 1943 he took a trip to
Portugal, a neutral country, where he would tour around the cities, meet his
fans, take in the sights and highlight the current war situation.

On 1 June 1943 his tour was over and he was booked on KLM/BOAC
flight 777, a Douglas DC-3, named *Ibis*, which was scheduled to fly from
the capital, Lisbon, back to England where it was due to land in Bristol
later that day. The aircraft had done this journey many times and the route

did not take it over any dangerous places. At no point was the aircraft thought to be at risk from the enemy.

However, the same aircraft had previously been on a similar route and had been attacked on two separate occasions by Luftwaffe aircraft, the pilots only escaping due to using evasive manoeuvres.

The plane carrying Leslie Howard took off at 0735 GMT with thirteen passengers on board and a crew of four, soon finding itself heading out to sea and turning towards the British Isles. It was in regular radio contact with Whitchurch Airport, its final destination. However, at around 1254 BST, Whitchurch was concerned by messages reporting that the aircraft was being followed and had been fired on. The coded messages read: 'An unidentified aircraft follows me. ... I am attacked by enemy aircraft.'

Looking at the evidence. from later accounts on the German side a *staffel* of eight Junkers Ju 88 C.6s from KG (Coastal Group) 40 were on patrol over the Bay of Biscay. Their tasks were air-sea-rescue and the protection of two U-boats. The Ju 88s spotted the DC-3 and attacked it, opening fire on *Ibis*. The attack was pressed home, an engine was hit and a wing caught fire. The airmen reported that three people exited the plunging aircraft but the parachutes did not open as they were on fire. The airliner crashed into the sea in the Bay of Biscay 200 miles north-west of Spain and sank. There were no survivors.

Next day, a Short Sunderland flying boat of 461 Squadron RAAF searched the area of the crash site in the hope that perhaps there had been a miracle and maybe it had ditched and everyone got out alive. But this was not to be. Instead, eight Ju 88s attacked the Sunderland in a very determined way. In spite of the Australian crew taking evasive action, low ever the waves, the Luftwaffe airmen continued to dive on the flying boat as it made its way northward to the UK. In the course of the forty-five-minute battle, Sunderland shot down at least three of the attackers. When the Germans broke off, five of the Sunderland's crew had been wounded, one of them fatally. The flying boat was able to reach its base in Cornwall in spite of some 500 bullet holes in the hull and wings.

Subsequently, flights to and from Lisbon were be re-routed and changed to night-time travelling to prevent this happening again. The film industry was in shock at the death of Leslie Howard. The loss of the aircraft made headlines around the world as his name was cemented into history as a film-star hero. Conspiracies were rife, many truly believing that the aircraft was shot down because German intelligence believed that Prime Minister

Winston Churchill was on the flight. The high-levels of German activity over the Bay before the shooting down of *Ibis* and the determined attack on the 461 Squadron Sunderland next day support this theory.

Another theory puts Howard down as a spy and that the shooting down was an actual targeting of the actor for assassination. This also held up when it came to the fact that he may have been killed as a symbol of Britain: kill Howard and the national morale goes with it – plus, the propaganda on the German side would be monumental. German officials in neutral countries alleged that Howard was 'on a secret mission'.

The ironic part of this is that, on the same day that Leslie Howard died in a plane crash, the name of another air-crash victim appeared in the same issue of *The Times*, that of Major William Martin. However, this latter report was completely false: William Martin didn't exist. Instead, the dead body of a homeless man was set adrift off Spain with 'secret documents' referring to a plan to invade Greece. This was a huge ruse that caused the Germans to move troops out of Sicily, the real target.

So, the world lost a famous movie star and a well-loved one at that. The star of *Romeo and Juliet* and *Gone with the Wind* was lost forever, his body never recovered and the aircraft at the bottom of the Bay of Biscay.

Chapter 51

Glenn Miller

One of the most famous musicians of the modern age was Glenn Miller with his band. He was a man whose music resonates through the ages and is still heard today and recognised, the most easily recognised being the famed *Glenn Miller Medley* which is loved around the world. But Glenn Miller was not just a musician, he was a member of the wartime effort to increase morale and install a sense of happiness in the troops about to head overseas, his band giving everyone who heard it that boost that said 'you're going, but you're coming back to this' kind of feeling.

Born on 1 March 1904 in Nebraska, USA, Miller gained an interest in music while just a teenager – like many other kids at school – only this spark ignited a passion that continued on long past graduation. Pursuing a career in music, he studied the tunes of the classical composers, learning the trombone along the way and performing wherever he could, much to the delight of his audiences.

Over time he became better at what he did and people started to recognise his name. He composed more and, by the late 1920s, had his own band that fed the American obsession with jazz and swing. Experimenting with a variety of instruments, Miller produced a unique sound, almost like a voice from within the noise, one that was becoming recognisable as his signature.

Performing with a band made his mark on the music industry undeniable. Becoming more popular, by the late 1930s his hard work had truly paid off, with his name on the posters as the star act and appearances in Hollywood films. But it was the outbreak of the Second World War that led to Glenn Miller having a change in his career, for he joined the US Army voluntarily.

Taking a huge pay cut, he joined a band and became accepted to entertain the troops with music and dance, being promoted to the rank of captain and then major by August 1944. Despite the war, his music was going really well; he was the most famous musician in the whole world at this point, partly due to his own style of swing and tunes that he simply put his name to.

His skills as a composer, musician and band leader earned him the position as leader of a marching band, broadcasting weekly on the radio and ending up with a fifty-piece band that took him to England in the summer of 1944 to record music at Abbey Road Studios. Life really was great for Glenn Miller and his musical genius.

His broadcasts were being used for both entertainment and propaganda, speaking over the music to talk about the war and promoting the beauty of music during a period of extreme conflict. While he was in London a bomb landed a few streets away from where the band was staying at the BBC Radio offices. The band departed for Bedford and the following day the entire building was destroyed in an air raid, killing around seventy people, including many with whom he had worked.

On 15 December 1944, Miller boarded a single-engine Noorduyn UC-64 Norseman for a trip from RAF Twinwood Farm in Clapham, London to Parisr. On board were two US Army officers, including the pilot. The aircraft gained height and turned towards the French coast. It was never seen again.

Nine days later it was announced that the plane carrying Glenn Miller had gone missing over the English Channel. At first it was just said that he would not be playing the Christmas Show on the BBC, but soon it became obvious that one of the most talented musicians of the war was never coming back.

Various theories over what happened were raised, but one in particular holds more than the rest. After watching the film *The Glenn Miller Story*, a former RAF navigator came forward and suggested that it was possible that his aircraft was nearby at the time of the crash. He noted in his log at the time that an aircraft matching Miller's flight at the same date and time was accidently hit by bombs that were dropped into the Channel following an aborted bombing mission. Aircraft were required to ditch ordnance in 'jettison areas' before landing and it seems that it just so happened that right underneath this particular aircraft was the UC-64 carrying Glenn Miller. Apart from this, the most held theory is that mechanical failure and bad weather brought the aeroplane down. The chances of survival in a December Channel would have been very slim, although no radio reports confirm that his aircraft was suffering from any difficulty. As it stands, the bomb jettison theory could be the answer. If this is true, then it certainly explains the disappearance and is much more plausible than the later conspiracies of Miller being on a secret mission or assassinated.

Following his disappearance, the legacy of Glenn Miller lived on through his music. Not only did he have the film about his life, but an official Glenn Miller Band was formed which still tours today, playing his greatest works. The Glenn Miller Orchestra for both the UK and Europe entertains people across the world, recording albums and performing for crowds all through the year.

Miller died leaving a widow and two stepchildren. They and his family have made sure his name lives on, societies formed in his honour and plaques appeared at places where he stayed and his name is today used on many different organisations that promote music and community get-togethers.

As for the missing aircraft, reports reached the press in 2019 that TIGHAR had been involved in attempting to identify an aircraft wreck found off the south coast of England and that, just thirty miles from land, all signs pointed to this being the missing aircraft. However, nothing was confirmed and the wreckage snagged by fishermen was reported elsewhere to be 150 miles from land and well away from where the aircraft would have been. Although TIGHAR have expressed interest in the search for Glenn Miller's plane, it still remains to be seen if it would be possible to find such a small craft in such a large area that is already littered with other aircraft, shipwrecks and, of course, thousands of pieces of Second World War ordnance.

He may have died in the Second World War in unexplained circumstances but the Glenn Miller name will live on for a long time yet. He was a great musician and, as history shows, also a great man.

Chapter 52

Flight 19

Whenever a book is written about the mysteries of the Bermuda Triangle, one subject in particular takes precedence over the rest and that is the disappearance of Flight 19. What is strange about this is that this was not one aircraft, it was a flight of five.

The Second World War had ended only three months previously but the US military was still keeping up with regular training, for the world was still very much a fragile place. On 5 December 1945 Lieutenant Charles Taylor was leading a team of five Grumman TBM Avenger torpedo-bombers on a training exercise to test navigation skills off the Florida coast, conduct dummy bomb attacks and then head back via Grand Bahama Island over which they would fly.

The small fleet would consist of a total of fourteen men, three in four of the aircraft and two in the last machine. Each pilot had a decent amount of flying time to his name already, so this should not have been anything that they couldn't handle.

The five aircraft took off from Fort Lauderdale at the US Naval Air Station at around 1410 hours, their planes heading out together to conduct the plan of attack, named Navigation Problem No 1, which was carried out, as expected, without any problems. This particular exercise was one scheduled throughout the day for several other teams as part of the continuous training that US Navy pilots were subjected to when not in combat.

The only problem with the aircraft was the lack of time-pieces, some of which were missing, but each pilot was assumed to have a watch, so this was not a cause for concern. With the exercise successfully completed at around 1500 hours, the five bombers turned back towards Fort Lauderdale. Everything seemed fine and, while they were inbound, another group was forming up ready to conduct the same exercise.

Then a strange radio transmission began. Somebody asked one of the students, Captain E.J. Powers, for a compass reading, his reply seemed confused: 'I don't know where we are. We must have got lost after that last turn.'

The group forming up was led by instructor Lieutenant Robert Fox who transmitted back to Powers: 'This is FT-74, plane or boat calling Powers, please identify yourself so someone can help you.'

The reply was not to Fox but to the other members of the Flight 19 crews. Captain Taylor came over the radio: 'FT-28, this is FT-74, what is your trouble?'

'Both of my compasses are out and I am trying to find Fort Lauderdale, Florida. I am over land but it's broken. I am sure I'm in the Keys but I don't know how far down and I don't know how to get to Fort Lauderdale.'

It seemed that confusion was starting to get the better of the flight since no IFF (Identification, Friend or Foe) signal could be picked up and no bearings could be obtained on the aircraft. Transmissions were still being received but they were not making much sense; orders to change course for a certain period of time and then head west, a clear difference in what some of the pilots thought they should do but some may not have wanted to speak up.

By then the weather was getting bad and the aircraft were estimated to be around 200 miles out to sea. They were heading towards Florida, apparently, so would be going '270 degrees west until landfall or running out of gas' with constant communications with the air station. By 1750 hours the radio stations had triangulated the aircraft to being within a 100 mile radius, but time was ticking on. The sun had already set by the time Taylor radioed again, at 1804, to say that he hadn't flown far enough east and needed to turn to fly east again. Fifteen minutes later the last message was received from Taylor: 'All planes close up tight … we'll have to ditch unless landfall … when the first plane drops below ten gallons, we all go down together.'

This message alone was concerning enough to sound the alarm that the five aircraft were soon to ditch in the sea. The first aircraft to take off in a search, just after 1800 hours and before the final messages had been received, was a Consolidated Catalina flying boat. After sunset two Martin PBM-5 Mariners were ordered out from their own training exercises to search for the five missing aircraft.

One of them took off at 1927 hours with thirteen people on board. It was hoped that the aircraft would be able to conduct a search of the seas off Florida with a good chance of locating any survivors and, if possible, conducting a rescue.

But Flight 19 was nowhere to be seen. If the aircraft had been where they were supposed to be then they would have seen Florida and its coastline with no problem, but it seemed that they were out at sea for hours with no clue as to where the land was. The rules stated that if anyone who was lost should head on a direction of 270 degrees which would eventually lead to land where they could get their bearings and find the way home. What went wrong with five aircraft was anybody's guess.

As the search continued through the night one of the Martin Mariners failed to return to base. Just after 2100 hours, the aircraft carrier USS *Solomons* reported suddenly losing radar contact with an aircraft at the exact time and location that a tanker reported an explosion and flames out at sea. A search of the area found no survivors.

The search for the six aircraft went on for almost a week but they found not a thing that would give any clue as to the fate of the twenty-seven crew, nor where they had last been. An inquiry found that nothing conclusive could be pinpointed other than bad weather and confusion being a factor.

Since the mystery first came about there has been speculation as to where the aircraft had crashed/ditched. Since the 1980s, when deep sea technology was getting more readily available, there were more and more claims of Flight 19 wreckage being found, only to be discounted later upon further research. Some claims could not be discounted as coming from the famous vanished flight but at the same time they couldn't be confirmed. In just a few years Fort Lauderdale had lost a total of ninety-five people in crashes, the seabed off Florida littered with the remains of aircraft and their crews.

In one expedition in 1991 five Avengers were found. This caused huge excitement, but when the aircraft were examined it was found that the numbers on at least one corresponded to a crash two years before Flight 19. The five Avengers had all crashed at different times and, by coincidence, had ended up with all of them in one small area. What were the chances?

Today there is still no real answer to what happened to Flight 19 and the Martin Mariner. The mystery is as deep today as it was in 1945. This will continue to fascinate historians and conspiracy hunters for as long as it remains unsolved, but somewhere out at sea off the Florida coast is the answer that they have been waiting for.

Chapter 53

Flying Tiger Flight 739

On 14 March 1962 a Lockheed L-1049 Super Constellation took off from Travis Air Force Base in California carrying ninety-three United States Army Rangers, three South Vietnamese soldiers and eleven civilian crew members. The four-engine airliner, designated N6921C, was chartered by the military to transport the ninety-six passengers to their final destination of South Vietnam to relieve troops there who were training Vietnamese military to fight the Viet Cong guerrillas.

Anderson Air Force Base on Guam was the third of four stops along the way on a journey that would take two days to complete. The plane had already stopped at Honolulu where flight attendants complained about the state of the crew rest areas, and Wake Island where those flight attendants changed over with four others. Their next destination was Clark Air Base in the Philippines but, by the time the aircraft had landed in Guam, there was some minor engine maintenance to carry out which delayed take off.

The aircraft itself was operated by Flying Tiger Line but ran as Military Air Transport Service (MATS) flight 739, piloted by Captain Gregory Thomas. The plane taxied down the runway as normal and took off, heading to its next refuelling stop around eight hours' flying time away. The aircraft had more than enough fuel and at 1422 hours on 15 March the pilot gave a routine update via radio and said that his position was 280 nautical miles west of Guam.

Just over an hour later, following some radio interference due to static, Guam radioed Flying Tiger 739 again for an updated position, but there was no reply. Several attempts to contact the aircraft were met with silence. The weather was clear and the seas calm; there was nothing to suggest that the aircraft had been in any kind of trouble.

The following morning, the 16th, the Clark Field Rescue Co-ordination Centre declared the aircraft officially missing and every available resource was called in to help search for it. Every ship and aircraft was diverted to assist in the search operation. Due to the large amount of units in the area the coverage was immense.

But four days of searching found not a trace of the aircraft. The chance of finding any survivors was fading by the hour. After four more days, the search was officially called off. Over 200,000 square miles of ocean had been scoured but nothing had been found.

Straightaway, questions were being asked when it was revealed that, on 14 March, another similar aircraft chartered by the military had also met with disaster. That second aircraft suffered from some kind of difficulties just hours after taking off and crashed in the Aleutian Islands. This could mean that both aircraft were sabotaged and made to crash at around the same time. Flying Tiger Line discounted the theory and put it down as just a coincidence.

Another report from a tanker, the Liberian registered *TL Lenzen*, in mid-ocean said that the crew had seen vapour trails in the sky and as the trails passed behind clouds a huge explosion got the crew's attention as it turned into reddish orange light. What followed was two flaming objects of equal brightness falling straight down. The ship's radar picked the objects up so they knew they were not seeing things. It was seventeen miles away, so the ship turned around to intercept the falling objects and see what was going on.

When the tanker headed to the area the crew found nothing in the sea, but continued looking for almost six hours before calling off their search. There was simply nothing there. Attempts to contact US Navy radio stations were met with silence, so they assumed at the time that it was an exercise of some kind and thought nothing more of it. A note was made of the time and positions, although in the absence of any other evidence, it is possible that this actually was the aircraft exploding in flight.

This lost aircraft has not gained much attention, the loss of 107 people on a civilian aircraft being just one of many air disasters of the 1960s. With this one carrying military personnel, the US Army was hit hard, especially with the Vietnam campaign. Over ninety people were missing in their area of operations.

Sixty years later a memorial was placed in South Portland, Maine, to honour those who never returned from the flight that vanished. In 2021, Senator Gary Peters introduced a Senate Bill that would add the names of the missing soldiers on the Vietnam Memorial. At the time of writing that is still under consideration.

No wreckage or bodies were ever found. An investigation drew a blank and had to rely on the witnesses out at sea to give at least some kind of explanation of what may have happened. Flying Tiger ceased to exist in the 1980s after being bought out by FedEx.

But, six decades on, the fate of Flying Tiger 739 remains a mystery.

Chapter 54
MH370

Of all the disappearances in the world and throughout history, there have been none so strange as that of the 2014 loss of a modern jet airliner with over 200 people on board. That loss occurred in circumstances so out of the ordinary that an investigation still continues. Malaysian Airlines Flight MH370 eclipsed Amelia Earhart as the number one aviation mystery of all time and, as the years went by, it seemed that more questions were being asked than actually answered.

The aircraft involved was a Boeing 777-200ER, registration 9M-MRO, which was first flown in 2002, being delivered brand new to Malaysian Airlines in May that year. The total number of passengers that the aircraft could carry was 282, plus the usual crew of around a dozen to look after the needs of the passengers.

The Boeing 777 has always had a good safety record. Three previous incidents had occurred over the years, including the very public crash landing of a British Airways flight at Heathrow Airport in 2008 where the crew skilfully brought the aircraft down after ice caused fuel starvation; all 152 people on board were alive although there were some injuries. But, as far as airliners go, this was a popular aircraft to be on and it was well liked since the design was first brought into the world in the early 1990s.

On 7 March 2014 the airliner was loaded up at Kuala Lumpur International Airport in Malaysia with 227 passengers and twelve crew for the scheduled trip to the Chinese capital Beijing. Doing checks within the cockpit were the pilot, 53-year-old Captain Zaharie Shah and co-pilot, 27-year-old First Officer Fariq Hamid, both of whom had many thousands of hours of flying experience. This was a regular journey, although Hamid's flight was his last training flight before he was due to take an examination for his qualification to make him a confirmed First Officer on Boeing 777s.

The flights from Malaysia to China were regular, the airline offering twice daily crossings each morning, a journey lasting just over five and a half hours long. At 0042 hours Malaysian time on 8 March, MH370 took off from Runway 32R and immediately ascended to 18,000 feet en route to

Beijing. The passengers and crew settled into their routine and everything seemed to be going fine. Minutes later the flight was cleared to climb to 35,000 feet which they confirmed over the radio at 0101 hours.

An automatic position report was sent using ACARS – the Aircraft Communications Addressing and Reporting System – which fed data about the flight's systems and fuel consumption back to a receiver. At 0119 hours Lumpur radar made their last voice transmission with the flight:

Lumpur Radar: 'Malaysian three seven zero, contact Ho Chi Minh one two zero decimal nine. Good night.'

Flight 370: 'Good night. Malaysian three seven zero.'

They would contact air traffic control as they passed over Vietnamese air space but, when Ho Chi Minh City attempted to contact MH370, they couldn't reach it. Another aircraft attempted to contact the flight on their behalf but got only static and what sounded like mumbling. A satellite data unit was still giving details of the flight automatically, but nobody could raise the flight on the radio.

At 0120 hours MH370 disappeared from radar screens at Kuala Lumpur while over the Gulf of Thailand. Seconds later Ho Chi Minh lost it. The two air traffic controls track aircraft by the use of a transponder carried on the aircraft, known as secondary radar, which meant that the transponder on board the Boeing 777 had stopped working suddenly. Normally, this would mean that an aircraft had met with some kind of event such as a crash, but then strange things started to happen.

Military radar still had the plane and was tracking the airliner, but could see that the plane had turned right and was heading in a completely different direction, going south-west away from China. The altitude was read as between 31,000 and 33,000 feet and it was also detected on several civilian radars along the way. At 0152 hours the airliner flew across the Strait of Malacca and passed south of Penang. In the meantime, air traffic controls around Asia were talking to each other about the bizarre behaviour of the flight and trying to find a way to contact the aircraft. Tracking the Boeing 777 was becoming difficult with the transponders not being on and much of the time was spent guessing where the plane was, based on its then current trajectory.

At 0225 hours the airliner's satellite communications system sent a 'log on request' message and transferred data back to the ground stations. This system logged several unanswered calls to the aircraft and responded to hourly status requests, the final transmissions from this system being at 0819 hours, almost two hours after the aircraft should have landed at Beijing. A status request at 0915 did not receive a response.

In the meantime, Malaysian Airlines issued a statement saying that contact with the aircraft had been lost and that a search and rescue operation had been launched. The missing plane did not report difficulties or weather problems, nor did it signal distress. The entire episode was so out of the ordinary that it was shocking.

Clearly the aircraft had not landed anywhere and so the assumption was that it had crashed with no survivors. The search area was nowhere near where the plane was meant to be. The radar had it heading towards the Indian Ocean, so the focus was going to be around there; the only problem was that this was a huge area and one that would not bring results quickly.

Within twenty-four hours the seas were busy with ships and aircraft from several countries, each hoping that they could find at least something that would tell them where the aircraft had gone down. There was always the hope that the aeroplane had ditched and that there were survivors, but the chances are never great even for such situations.

In the meantime, it was found that two passengers were not actually on board, their passports having been stolen and used by two Iranians who were probably migrants heading to Germany. Australia joined the search for the aircraft but, as the days turned into weeks with nothing to show for the search, concern was growing that this was bigger than anybody had thought previously.

With the aircraft underwater, the black box flight recorders would only send a transmission out on the locator beacon for around forty days maximum, so ships from all over were scouring the seabed listening for the ping. Again, nothing was found despite several false alarms. Sonobuoys deployed from military ships again heard nothing.

The weeks were turning into months, pieces of wreckage were found floating and were recovered only to be tested and discounted as being part of MH370. Time was ticking on and relatives wanted answers that the investigators couldn't provide. The only information they had was the data collected from the transmissions and radar pictures on the night.

Malaysian Airlines suffered another major blow on 17 July, less than four months later, when a second Boeing 777, designated MH17, was shot down over Ukraine during the conflict between that country and invading Russian forces. In that incident, 298 people were killed.

With no sign of anything to do with MH370, the seabed searches continued for several years, various survey ships running sonar scans across the bottom of the Indian Ocean. Incredibly, two historic shipwrecks were found and photographed along the way. But, on 29 July 2015, an object was found washed ashore on the island of Reunion in the western Indian Ocean. Examination of the piece found that it resembled part of an aircraft and over the coming days several other suspect aeroplane parts were found and sent for testing.

One of these pieces was a flaperon from a Boeing 777 wing. A number found on the piece confirmed 100 per cent that this had come from the lost MH370. Other parts found in the following months were also believed to be from the flight, but this gave no indication as to where those parts had come from. Trying to calculate how long they were drifting, how far they had travelled and how they ended up in that area still gave no conclusive answer as to where the aircraft was.

After three years of searching, the underwater survey teams were called off in January 2017 with nothing to show except where the aircraft wasn't. This was a disappointing result but the search will recommence if new evidence points to a specific area. With 46,000 square miles of seabed searched there was no point carrying on any further when the crash site could literally be anywhere.

The loss of MH370 continues to baffle investigators. Conspiracy theories are rife with nothing to say any of the claims are wrong. There is just nothing to say what the truth is other than the known facts, and those are few and far between.

What we do know is that the transponders were deliberately turned off and the aircraft turned onto a new course heading towards the Indian Ocean. There is no way to excuse this; it was deliberate and this decision cost 239 lives. Whatever happened onboard that aircraft we can only speculate. Never before has an aircraft literally vanished without trace. At least with the Flying Tiger flight a witness possibly saw the aircraft explode first. In the case of MH370, it was tracked on radar and then it suddenly dropped off.

But why would this deliberate act have taken place in the first place? Hijacking is one theory and it has happened before with the attacks on 11 September 2001 when hijackers took over the four planes, turning off the transponders and flying them into targeted landmarks. Another hijack in 1996 with an Ethiopian Airlines Boeing 767 saw the pilot tell the terrorists that the long-distance trip they wanted him to make was impossible because they didn't have enough fuel. Accusing the pilot of lying, they forced him to fly the aircraft. Thankfully, he flew it close to land and eventually was forced to crash land off the Comoros Islands where it broke up on impact, killing 125 people. There were survivors, thanks to the captain's thinking.

So hijacking was a possibility, but nobody has claimed responsibility for the attack if that is the case. Terrorists need people to know it was they who carried it out or it is pointless and their voices are not being heard. So that leads to the next alternative – that the people who crashed it were the air crew themselves. There are several instances during the jet airliner age when a pilot has flown the aircraft deliberately into the ground and killed all the passengers and crew. In 2015, Germanwings flight 9525 slammed into a mountain in the Alps, killing all 150 people onboard. When the investigators found the true cause, the pilot had locked himself in the cockpit alone and aimed the Airbus A320 into the ground. This disaster was not the first and most likely won't be the last, so it is not too far-fetched to think that this could be a cause. The question would be: who on the plane had carried out this act of mass murder?

As it stands, the mystery of the loss of MH370 is just as unexplained today as it was when the aircraft first made the alteration of course. The wreckage wasn't found but wreckage found the shore. Already there are books written about this disaster, TV series and documentaries exploring the myths and the facts to try to make some kind of sense of what happened to the 239 people onboard and why a modern jet airliner could simply fly into oblivion in the technology age of the twenty-first century.

Epilogue

When I wrote this book I was hoping to add as many cases of things lost at sea as possible, I wanted to grip the reader with tales of mystery as well as tell the stories of the famous wrecks and relics that are still to be discovered. What was most difficult in the end was trying to choose which to add and which to leave out. So many fascinating stories with many different versions and aspects to the same tale. But what I did want to do was get to the truth in each case. We can safely say that Atlantis did not exist, but other places did which could have provided a base for the legend that grew.

The *Mary* (not Marry or Marie) *Celeste* was not found with a hot meal on the table and the fire still burning. It was missing the lifeboat and the contents of several barrels of alcohol. If anything, it is the disappearance of a lifeboat full of people that is more mysterious, for we know what became of the ship. But stories being retold by word of mouth or rumour become a hazy 'fact' and suddenly you have a completely different story.

How many people knew of the ships that were also found abandoned? The *High Aim 6, Kaz II, Jian Seng, Joyita* and the *Carroll A. Deering* were all just as mysterious if not more so. Even with modern-day evidence we cannot say for sure what happened to those crews, other than to examine what we have and go with the facts that are available (at the time).

Then we have the disappearance of entire ships, the *Cyclops* with over 300 people on board, the *Naronic* with seventy-four, *Pacific* with 189, *Hans Hedtoft* with ninety-five; the list goes on, each ship leaving behind very little information as to its fate. Some had no wreckage located by search teams whatsoever but that doesn't mean there was none – just that none had been found.

This brings us on to the myth of the Bermuda Triangle, an area that has seen more ships and aircraft disappear than anywhere else in the world. But most of these incidents can be explained, especially with the recent discoveries of some of the ships that had been claimed by the so-called Triangle. The loss of the *Cyclops* is, in all fairness, a huge mystery, but one has to look at the bigger picture, such as sea conditions at the time and the state of the ship, not to mention that no serious major expedition has ever been launched to search for half of these missing ships. *Marine Sulphur Queen* obviously went down due to some kind of catastrophic event with wreckage bearing her name located soon after. Flight 19 and the Martin Mariner flying boat clearly encountered some kind of weather problem that disorientated the crews and caused them to crash, in the case of the Avengers after most likely running out of fuel.

The ocean floor is littered with shipwrecks and lost aircraft, but it is fair to say that the aircraft carrying people such as Glenn Miller and Amy Johnson are unlikely to be found and identified. An aircraft on the seabed during a war would be one of dozens; the only way to identify each one would be with the serial numbers, many of which will now be unreadable, if they are found at all. There may be a chance to find Amelia Earhart due to the aircraft being unique for the area where she went missing – and the fact that her last flight can be narrowed down to a specific area – although it is still a huge area.

Two airliners over fifty years apart still remain to be found, both Flying Tiger 739 and Malaysian Airlines 370 are still missing, although how the latter remains lost is something that has had many people concerned for years now and rightly so.

So, out of all the lost things in this book, how many of them can be found in this day and age? Well, the first part is a definite no – the chances of locating people over a hundred years after they vanish from a lighthouse or a ship at sea is so low that it is not even worth searching for a figure. Unless new evidence appears of a mysterious body washing up on a shore and given a burial so that it can be exhumed and identified as coming from one of those incidents, those cases are well and truly closed and will remain mysteries.

Out of all the aircraft cases, the two airliners and, possibly, the airship *Italia* have more of a chance than the rest. Robert Ballard still aims to hunt for Amelia Earhart's aeroplane, so only time will tell if that search is successful.

But what of the shipwrecks that are today lost at sea? There is more chance of finding the ones that went down with eyewitnesses than there is of those that vanished without trace. Attempting to locate the *Pacific* or *Baychimo* may end up with a search area of tens of thousands of square miles, but the location of a ship going under during the war would have more of a chance.

Ships like HMS *Barham*, HMS *Kelly*, the USS *Oklahoma* and the *Californian* all had other ships around them at the time, in many cases Allied ships noting their positions, as well as any nearby enemy ship that was attacking them at the time. Cross referencing those positions defines a relatively narrow search area. When the German battleship *Bismarck* was sunk by the Royal Navy in 1941 there were dozens of ships involved, each giving accurate positions, but each was slightly different from the other. It still took Ballard two attempts to find the wreck. His search for *Titanic* eventually located the wreckage thirteen miles away from where she reported her position to be. Thirteen miles on the sea is a huge area to be out when checking positions.

So out of every ship in this book, which ones will somebody consider a search for? Which would be worth the millions of dollars in hiring out a ship and underwater detection equipment just to say that they had found it? The *Royal Merchant* could repay that reward but is just as hard to find, if not harder, than any other.

Let's face facts. Unless there is a huge historical importance linked to a ship, nobody is going to front up an expedition just to bring back images for a book that, when sold, would not cover the cost. Microsoft co-founder Paul Allen had billions of dollars, so when he died and asked for his money to be spent on tracking down shipwrecks from the Second World War, the world was given a unique legacy to have final resting places confirmed for many of the most important shipwrecks that had not been discovered.

How many of these are important enough today? The *Bonhomme Richard* stands a good chance of a search, *F4* may soon be located if the Royal Navy continue to scour the seabed of Choiseul Sound with sonar. The same could be said for the *Kelly*, *Californian* and *Waratah*, the historic value of the ship making a good TV programme and justifying the cost. But who would want to put up money to search for the two missing trawlers from Hull that remain to be found?

Every single ship wrecked in this book deserves its story to be told and it is hoped that one day each one will be found, the story re-told and the victims honoured as they should be. When a wreck is found it solves the mysteries but sometimes opens up new ones. HMS *Perseus* was one story: sunk off Greece, the only survivor told a tale of escaping from around 150 feet down, but not before he had finished off a bottle of rum for Dutch courage. When surfacing he swam several miles to the shore where he later told his epic story of survival. Some didn't believe him, but when the wreck was found in 1997 divers found an open hatch with an empty rum bottle underneath, thus proving his story true.

Stories of the ships that came to grief will continue to fascinate, whether it is because of the lure of gold and treasure, the stories of its heroes or because of the mystery surrounding the vessel and its final hours. The *General Grant* and *Merchant Royal* are two that are still missing, loaded with riches, yet carrying the story of the crews who went down with them. When treasure ships are found it is a wonder how many people think of these people as they focus on the monetary value.

There were several wrecks that should have been in here, but as the book was being written there were news reports on a number of those important shipwrecks being confirmed as located, one of them being the *Griffon*, a sailing vessel sunk in the Great Lakes in 1679. She was built by famous French explorer Rene-Robert Cavelier, Sieur de La Salle, and for years there had been articles about the discovery of a wreck that could be the *Griffon*, the questions of 'was it/wasn't it?' going back and forth. Eventually, in 2022, carbon dating proved that a wreck located in 2018 was in fact the *Griffon*.

I toyed with the idea of putting two Russian submarines in, *K-129* and *K-219*, both sunk through accident and both nuclear powered. But one was already located and had a secret salvage attempt and the other is monitored for radiation and so the locations are known roughly anyway.

This book lacks American warships thanks to recent events and several major discoveries of the USS *Lexington*, *Indianapolis*, *Hornet*, *Nevada*, *Johnston* and *Wasp* to name but a few. Several major Japanese warships have been found from the Pacific campaign; the big ones such as *Yamato* and *Musashi* were found, as were the major Australian ones. British warships seem to be the most elusive. *Hood* was found, as was *Ark Royal*, *Hermes* and Franklin's lost Arctic ships *Erebus* and *Terror*. But the carriers *Glorious* and *Courageous*, battleship *Barham* and dozens of frigates and destroyers remain lost to this day. These are all amazing ships with incredible stories, stories that need telling before they are lost to history once more.

You have to admire those who go searching for these historic relics for they do not just provide fascinating historical insight but give closure to those who were personally involved in the sinking. Giving a Second World War veteran a chance to see his ship once again is priceless. To capture those stories for posterity makes it all worthwhile. For this we wish the explorers of the world the best of luck and hope that they continue with their successes for the future searches.

For over three decades I have buried myself in books and been to more libraries than I have drunk in pubs, but this pastime of mine has led me to find fascinating historical context over the years. I have climbed the cliffs of Anguilla to get photos of wrecked ships, visited museums across the world, explored two of the diving world's top ten shipwrecks (*Zenobia* and *Bianca C*) and written about all this, plus more, in my books. I was proud to say that I spent many years researching the sinking of the destroyer HMS *Duchess* to bring that story to light, the *SRN6-012* hovercraft, tanker *Pacific Glory* and the wrecks of the Great Gale of 1871. There will always be a shipwreck to study and write about.

While writing this the news came through of the discovery of HMS *Gloucester*, sunk off Norfolk in 1682, and two ships near the wreck of the recently discovered treasure ship *San Jose* off Colombia. It seems that each year new and exciting discoveries are being made that will add to our understanding of the history of the maritime world and provide us with answers that we didn't even know we were looking for.

I said at the beginning that the discovery of *Endurance* made my most recent book *The 50 Greatest Shipwrecks* already out of date. I would very much like this book to be out of date just as quick and for the same reasons, that of new and exciting discoveries.

Acknowledgements

I t is hard to thank all the people who assist me when I write a book but I do like to take the time to try; I believe it is only fair when help goes acknowledged. Firstly, I would like to pay tribute to my wife for the many hours that we are in the same room but I am hard at work researching; not once does she complain and yet for every result good or bad she is there to tell me what a great job I'm doing. While I am away, she is there at home saving me news articles, recording things off the TV and taking messages that will keep feeding my archive of material that has been building up for over three decades. This is a way of life that will never get old for me and I hope you get just as much interest out of it as I do. Thank you to you my darling Juliette.

To the libraries and archives around the world, without whose dedicated staff and collectors there would be no material to write books with, nor will there be a place in which to read such books. I would like to thank the National Archives in Kew, East Riding Archives and libraries at Bridlington, Portsmouth, Southampton, Plymouth, Hull, and London, to name just a few.

To the fellow authors who have provided a wealth of information in the past which has led me to decide which shipwrecks to write about. Brian Lavery's brilliant book on the Triple Trawler disaster, *The Headscarf Revolutionaries*, was a definite page-turner and one that opened my eyes as to the real story of the fight for trawler safety. Obviously very well researched and full of information, this is a definite recommended read. To the huge amount of information online, words cannot express my admiration for the people who continue to feed historical information into these sites and update them for people like me to read. These pages keep the history alive and, in many cases, prevent it from being forgotten. Keep up the good work!

I'd like to thank those who spoke to me about the missing landing craft *Foxtrot 4*, the families of Dusty and Rob who are still mourned by their sisters forty years on yet still keep their memory alive. I hope one day I can write about this landing craft on its own and bring the full story to light.

Most of all I would like to thank the readers of my work. Without you there would be no point to writing and the feedback I get is always welcomed. If you enjoyed the read, leave a review, if you find mistakes then tell me; I am never too proud to admit an error and will correct any where I am able.

This will not be my last book; in fact there is already a list of projects being worked on for the future. If I have brought any of these stories to light enough to keep it remembered then this book has served its purpose.